BOOKMARKED FOR BLOOD

A Bookish Cafe Mystery Book 5

HARPER LIN

Chapter 1

Two women loitered at the register, chattering away at a rate of at least three hundred words a minute. At least, that was what Maggie Bell thought as she hid behind the tall bookshelves in the children's corner of the Bookish Café. On and on the women nattered about how wonderful they looked and how they hadn't changed a bit and had they heard about so-and-so and whatever happened to such-and-such and remember the blah-blah-blah during home-coming and wasn't that just so much fun.

Maggie took a deep breath as she peeked around the shelf. Her eye just happened to fall on an old copy of *Trixie Belden and the Mystery of the Slinking Shadow*. The irony made her pinch her lips together before carefully peeking at the women again. It was as if she'd been hiding for hours. Why didn't they at least go to the café and take a seat instead of rambling on about their days in high school by the bookshelves?

"What are you doing?"

The deep male voice shocked Maggie, almost making her yelp. She clapped her hand over her own mouth before any sound came out and turned to face her boss. She put a finger to her lips.

"Maggie, are you aware that Valentine's Day is just around the corner and we don't have our window display up yet?" whispered Joshua Whit-field, the owner of the Bookish Café.

"Yes," Maggie whispered back. "As soon as those women leave, I'll get started on it."

"Why are you waiting for those women to leave?"

"Because I don't want to talk to them," she replied.

"Why not?" Joshua crouched slightly, like Maggie was doing, trying to remain unseen.

"I went to high school with them. They are in town for the reunion. A reunion, can you believe that? The whole thing makes me feel itchy."

"Is that all?" Joshua finally straightened up and looked down a couple inches at Maggie.

She straightened too, and she could tell by Joshua's smirk that he didn't understand her angst at all. But there was absolutely no need for him to look so handsome while missing her point completely.

"Is that all? It's *too* much. For the past week, I've been shucking and jiving in and out of doorways, behind bushes, and under tables just to avoid the invasion of classmates who have been popping up all over town." She shuddered.

"Why? You visit with so many of them every day. Didn't you and Gary go to school together?" Joshua replied.

His inquiry annoyed Maggie because he was totally right.

"I don't visit with them. I *tolerate* them."

As she was trying to explain her discomfort with strolling down memory lane without going into great detail about her awkward and embarrassing high school experience, her two classmates left the bookstore. She looked to the door as the jingling bell indicated movement and finally let out a long sigh.

"You can't hide from every customer that comes

in. I don't know why you'd want to. You practically run this bookstore. Our window displays win almost every competition Fair Haven has because they are so beautiful and creative. And you look like you could still be in high school. Isn't that what you girls are always worried about? Who got fat? Who went bald? You did neither," Joshua said with that adorable smirk that made Maggie want to melt.

She frowned and rolled her eyes. "Very funny."

"I'm being serious," Joshua said.

For a second, they stood there in awkward silence. Had this been a movie or romance novel, Maggie was sure he would have scooped her into his arms and they would have shared a beautiful first kiss. But this was real life, and instead, Maggie backed into the bookshelf, making *Horton Hears a Who* and *Red Fish, Blue Fish* fall to the floor. With both of them scrambling to pick up the books, a headbutt was inevitable. They stood, Maggie rubbing her left eyebrow as Joshua tenderly touched the right side of his forehead.

"Could you get away from me now?" Maggie huffed.

"Yes. I will. You're dangerous to be around, Maggie Bell," Joshua said. "And I'm waiting to see the window display. Valentine's Day is coming whether you like it or not. You're running out of time. Here." He reached around to retrieve his wallet.

Maggie, still rubbing her forehead, waited as he counted out one hundred dollars. "What's this for? Settling out of court?" she smirked.

"Go buy whatever you need for the window. Maybe pick up a couple of things for the café too. I know Babs has some ideas, so maybe ask her if there is anything she might be looking for." Joshua nodded before heading back into the storeroom.

Maggie blushed. She looked around the bookstore and realized that a lot had changed since Alexander Whitfield, Joshua's father, had run the place. She had worked for him for years, and there were times, like now, she really wished he were there to talk to. When he'd died, it was as if Maggie had lost her favorite warm sweater to a thief who ripped it from her shoulders before running away, laughing loudly.

"What would you say to him now, Maggie Bell? That you have a crush on his son and don't know what to do about it?" she muttered as she stacked the books back in their places.

The sad thing was she knew she wouldn't have had to tell Mr. Whitfield a thing about how she felt for Joshua. He'd have known without her uttering one single syllable. There would be that look in his eye that she'd seen a million times when he suggested she read a book at which she'd previously turned her nose up. Like the time he'd made her read *The Time Machine*.

"Ugh. I don't like science fiction," she had grumbled.

"You will enjoy this one. I know you will," Mr. Whitfield had insisted as he handed her the worn-out copy. "There is more to it than time travel."

She snatched the book away from him and clicked her tongue. "You remember I wasn't all that crazy for *War of the Worlds*. It just didn't stick with me. The old movie on Family Classics was better. H.G. Wells is just not…"

"Just not what? Romantic enough?" Mr. Whitfield teased.

"'Just not my cup of tea' is what I was going to say," Maggie replied. "All the descriptions of futuristic machines and the creatures that drive them seems to go on and on…and on." With a deliberate eye roll, she turned from her boss and tucked the book into her backpack to take home.

"At least give it a chance. Sometimes, an author doesn't get into his own voice until after a first book.

Sometimes, they lose their voice after a first book. Everyone deserves a second chance, don't you think?"

Maggie had always hated when Mr. Whitfield made her reconsider. Since reading was Maggie's favorite hobby, she had finished the book that night. When she had walked into the shop the next morning, Mr. Whitfield had had that look in his eyes that she loved and hated at the same time.

"Well? What did you think?" he asked as if he didn't know the answer.

"It was better than I thought it would be," Maggie reluctantly replied.

"Not just a science fiction story, now, was it?"

After a deep inhale and exhale, Maggie stomped up to her boss and handed him the book.

"No, it was wonderful and very moving in parts, and I hope you are happy knowing you are making me annoyed."

Mr. Whitfield chuckled, giving her that look that said he knew he was right. She'd seen that look a lot over the years. It made her smile even as tears stung her eyes. Mr. Whitfield had died at the bookstore while she was with him. One minute, they were talking about a book, and the next, everything was silent, as if a radio had been suddenly snapped off or a washing machine had finally finished its cycle. Not only had Mr. Whitfield died suddenly, but he had died peacefully in the place he loved the most with someone who thought of him as family. *Isn't that what everyone hopes for when their time comes?*

Maggie nodded at the memory. Quickly, she shook off the sadness, sniffled, and wiped her nose with her sleeve. By this time, the coast was clear and there was no sign of her classmates anywhere.

"Valentine's Day. Ugh," she muttered as she slipped into her coat and tucked the money Joshua had given her into her pocket.

She'd had a couple of ideas about how she wanted the display window to look. She wasn't sure they were as lovey-dovey as her boss may have wanted. She was sure that everywhere down the main drag, there would be silhouettes of cupids, red and pink hearts cut out of construction paper, and silly slogans like "Love is in the air" or that oldie but goodie, "Be my valentine," plastered in the windows. Those were the images to be avoided at all costs.

With her hood pulled over her head and her scarf wrapped across her nose, Maggie marched outside, confident that if she crossed paths with any of her classmates, they would not recognize her.

The wind had kicked up slightly since she'd arrived at work that morning. The sky had been a bright blue but was slowly turning overcast. Maggie always preferred gray days to sunny ones and took this to be a sign her day was going to get better and be free of any unwelcome visitors and conversations.

Of course, fate had other plans.

Chapter 2

Sell It Again Sam was an old elementary school that had been transformed into a gigantic thrift store off the beaten track of Main Street, tucked behind some of the most beautiful older homes in Fair Haven. Maggie was always surprised at the things people got rid of. She bought almost all of her vintage sweaters and jewelry there, and although she rarely spoke to anyone, the staff did all know her and gave her a friendly wave when she walked in. Today was no exception.

With a quick grin and wave, Maggie acknowledged the woman who was always working at the front register. Maggie wasn't sure, but she thought her name was Sadie. She looked like a Sadie. Leopard print was a staple in her wardrobe.

Normally, a trip to SIAS would require about two hours because Maggie would slowly meander from room to room. Each classroom was dedicated to a specific subject. One was women's clothes. Another was men's. There was a room full of children's toys and another full of books. Normally, Maggie spent most of her time searching through the stacks of vintage romances and collections that people had donated.

But today, she was on a mission and made her way to the holiday room. Christmas trees and jack-o'-lanterns were displayed side by side all year round. In addition to the big holidays, there were corners dedicated to St. Patrick, the miracle of Easter, and what Maggie was in search of: Valentine's Day décor. She spied elegant vintage cards, signed by mysterious individuals who Maggie imagined were separated by miles or maybe even forbidden lovers sending daring communications through the US Postal Service. The idea made her smirk, and she came up with a unique idea for the display window. It wasn't the traditional pink-and-red "Be mine" kind of décor. She'd leave Babs in the café. No, the bookstore was going to have a humdinger of a display. Maggie thought this might be her most creative idea yet.

She managed to scoop up two shoeboxes full of cards and grabbed some paper doilies and a few random bags of tiny sparkly red hearts that could be sprinkled on a table. A couple packs of vintage wrapping paper printed with bulging roses and delicate baby's breath also found their way into Maggie's basket.

Just as she was about to leave, feeling light and eager to get back to work, she ran smack into another woman, causing both of them to drop their treasures.

"I'm s-so sorry," Maggie stuttered.

"It never fails. When I'm in a hurry, something gets in my way," the woman replied.

Maggie couldn't tell if the lady was criticizing herself or blaming the collision on Maggie's clumsiness. As soon as she stood up and looked at the familiar face, though, she knew she was going to be one hundred percent to blame.

"Oh my gosh! Maggie Bell?" the woman gasped.

"Shelly Pinkowski?" Maggie muttered as if she had a slice of lemon in her mouth. She recognized the pug nose and heavy-lidded eyes that gave Shelly a continual look of indifference.

"Wow." Shelly stepped back and looked Maggie

up and down as if she was observing an animal in a zoo. "You haven't changed a bit."

"Yeah, neither have you," Maggie replied as she wrinkled her nose and pushed up her glasses. "I'm assuming you are here for the reunion?"

"Yes, well, sort of. My aunt passed away," Shelly said as if it was the most boring bit of news she could have to report.

"I'm so sorry," Maggie replied. It was what she had been raised to say when people reported bad news. It was what normal people did. But it proved to be unnecessary, since Shelly Pinkowski was not normal.

"She and my mother had a falling out years ago. I don't know what about. But I stayed in touch because, well, she had quite a bit of money, I'll be honest. And her own children had disowned her. That tells you something about my family, doesn't it?"

"Sort of," Maggie replied softly. She watched Shelly as if she was watching a movie on the verge of a jump scare.

"To make a long story short, she made me executor of her will. How about that? She also left everything to me, including that old, haunted house she lived in. You can bet I had that on the market as soon as I found out I owned it." Shelly smirked and shook her head.

"What house is that?"

"That big monstrosity on Campbell Street."

"You mean the one with the spires and the pillars in front?" Maggie asked.

She'd always loved that house and thought with a little paint and some landscaping, it would look like a life-size doll house.

"That's the one. Now, do I look like I could live in a house like that?" Shelly chuckled and flipped her hair. "I've got a house on the coast in California Wine Country. What do I need with a place that gets covered by ten feet of snow every winter?"

Maggie squinted at Shelly for a split second. Someone who hailed from the Golden State usually wasn't as pale as Maggie was. But maybe Shelly was tanless because she worked all the time or didn't like to sunbathe. Maybe she used SPF 2000 or something. As much as Maggie wanted to call bull on Shelly's story, she didn't. What would be the point?

"So, are you here for the reunion?" Shelly finally asked.

"I live in town. I've got a little place just... over..." Maggie started but stopped when she saw Shelly look at her watch.

"I'm sorry, Maggie. I really need to get going. I've had so much stuff dropped off here from the house, and I still have at least another truckload to deliver. I have to pack most of it myself. Heaven knows my cousins won't help."

"That's really sad that they won't even help with their mother's things," Maggie said. "Maybe it bothers them more than they are letting on. I lost someone close to me, and it was hard to go through his things." The thought of *not* helping pack up Mr. Whitfield's belongings was sinful to Maggie, and he hadn't even been related to her by blood.

"Please." Shelly waved her hand and rolled her eyes as she'd done a million times in high school at just about every comment made by anyone who was not in her little clique.

Maggie remembered wanting to slap her so hard her eyes would roll out onto the floor. That urge had not changed.

"Okay. Well... uhm... maybe..."

"If you are looking for some really old, really ugly furniture and tchotchkes, heaven awaits in the back." Shelly jerked her thumb over her shoulder. "I've got to get the rest of the junk out of that house, or else the real estate agent is going to have an episode. She insists I bake cookies so the house smells like sweets when people come to look at it. Do you believe that? Do I look like I bake anything?"

After Shelly flipped her hair again, Maggie just slowly shook her head and muttered "No. No, you don't."

"Now, *you* look like you bake lots of stuff. I think there are some cupcake tins and crazy bake pans in the shapes of bunches of grapes and stuff." Shelly laughed. "Hey, have fun. I'll see you at the reunion. We've got a lot to talk about."

Before Maggie could say anything, Shelly was already pushing her way through the thrifters toward the exit. It was useless to try to say goodbye, let alone explain that she probably wasn't going to see Shelly at the reunion. After this encounter, she had absolutely no desire to go.

With her Valentine's decorations in her hands, she turned in the direction of the registers, but curiosity got the better of her. "Really old, really ugly" had caught her attention, and she had to see what had been in Shelly's aunt's house.

As soon as she saw the stuff that was being priced and added to the shelves, she knew that not only had Shelly's attitude not changed, but she hadn't gotten any smarter after high school. The furniture pieces were lovely antiques. The knick-knacks might not have been worth money—no authentic Sister Maria Innocentia Hubble statues or rare Fabergé eggs—but the stuff was wonderfully kept, colorfully made, unique, and, in Maggie's eyes, beautiful.

Then she saw the stacks of books. Her heart leapt at the cloth-covered tomes and what looked like several sets of classics all bundled together. If only she had an hour or two, she'd sort through every title to grab herself a few gems. But she had to get back to work.

"Joshua did say to pick up a few things for Babs. She's not expecting anything really fancy," Maggie told herself as she inched closer to the stacks of books. The first title she saw convinced her that it wasn't just okay for her to take a few more minutes to review the inventory; it was necessary.

"*A Romance in Velvet*," she muttered. A book she'd never heard of. But didn't it sound romantic? She added it to her armful of goodies.

Before she knew it, forty-five minutes had passed, and she had half a dozen titles in with her Valentine's Day decorations. With a grunt, she pulled herself away from the pile, promising to come back in a day or two, and hustled to the register. With her lips pinched and her nose wrinkled, she bounced on her heels as she waited in line. Ahead of her was a woman haggling over the cost of a picture frame.

"I thought it said twenty-five cents," she whined to the nice lady in leopard print.

"No, ma'am. That says seventy-five cents."

"Well, I just… I don't know… I guess I'll take it." The tightwad sighed.

"How about we compromise and I'll only charge fifty cents." The leopard queen smiled happily.

Maggie thought that was a good deal and nodded in agreement.

"That sounds fine," replied the tightwad, who shrugged and nodded too.

Maggie didn't care what her treasures cost. She would pay with her own money and give Joshua his back. Since she had taken so long and bought extra things, she felt it was only fair. She smiled at the total of only six dollars for everything. With a quick push of her glasses up the nose, Maggie thanked the leopard queen and grabbed her stuff.

"Next week is half off everything, so make sure to come see us again," the woman said.

"I sure will," Maggie replied before hustling out the door.

She'd decided that since she was already late, a couple more minutes wouldn't make a difference. On the way back to the shop, she drove to Campbell Street. There was only one house with a U-Haul truck in the driveway and a Galloway Realty For Sale sign in the lawn. Maggie stopped the car and got out.

A Mercedes convertible was also parked on the street. At first, Maggie was sure it was Shelly's. Of course she drove a Mercedes up and down the coast from her fancy house in wine country.

"What do you care? You hate the sun," Maggie mumbled. She thought of the little home she rented. It wasn't much, but it was hers, decorated the way she liked and pretty from the outside.

She slowed her car, and as she did, she saw people in the driveway, along with a rather beat-up pickup truck parked close to the garage. That must have belonged to the groundskeeper. The property stretched back a good deal, and from what Maggie could see, there was a nice-sized backyard that probably needed tending.

"I am the only one doing anything!" Maggie heard.

"Miss Pinkowski, I told you what needed to be done to sell this house. Your aunt let many things go as the years went by. If you want to have a halfway decent chance of getting a fair price for this place, then you'll do as I'm telling you!" shouted another woman.

They were so loud Maggie could hear them through the closed windows of her car. It wasn't a warm day, but when it came to random arguments, Maggie would tolerate a little chill. And when an altercation involved an adversary from her high school days, she'd brave a blizzard in bare feet to get the scoop. She rolled the window down and pulled her car up behind the U-Haul. Pulling her hood and scarf around her face, she was sure she wouldn't be noticed.

"I told you I didn't care about the price! I want it off my hands," Shelly barked.

"Look, you might not realize the worth of this place, but I do! I'm not going to waste my time getting a bag of peanuts for something that…"

"This isn't your decision, Louise!"

"Miss Pinkowski, your name might have held a lot of water the last time you were in town. But since then, your stock has taken a dive, to say the least."

"How dare you talk to me…"

"I'm doing this as a favor. I know what happened when you went to California, and I know what's still going on. Shelly, you need all the help you can get, and that's what I'm trying to do. Help. I think…"

"How dare you!" Shelly shouted. "You're trying to help by keeping this monstrosity available when I know there have been offers. Who is paying the property tax and the utilities while I'm waiting? You sure the heck aren't!"

"None of those offers come close to what this place is worth. Shelly, be reasonable. I'm trying to help you and…"

"You're trying to screw me on this. Don't think I don't know why you're prolonging this. Fair Haven is a small town, and gossip is one of its favorite pastimes. Tell you what, Louise. Take your sign and your humanitarian efforts and shove them up your…" Just then, Shelly stopped talking.

Maggie, who had been watching the whole thing from a slouched position in her car, looked up to see Shelly glaring in her direction.

"Hey! Hey, you!" Shelly shouted and pointed to the car.

Maggie put it in gear and slowly pulled away,

keeping her eyes focused ahead of her and her back straight. Shelly yelled something else that Maggie could only partially make out. It included the words "*nosey*," "*mind*," and "*business*." But one thing was for sure: she didn't hear Shelly call out the name *Maggie*. So that was good enough.

Once back at the bookstore, she thought about what she'd heard on the driveway of Shelly's aunt's house. She wondered what the Realtor had been talking about when she'd said she knew what happened in California. What had Shelly meant by saying she knew why her Realtor was prolonging the sale? If gossip was Fair Haven's pastime, Maggie felt cheated. She had no idea what was going on and hadn't heard anything specific. But there had to be some loose lips somewhere.

Chapter 3

That night, as Maggie reached the front door of her home, she couldn't help but feel a little twinge of jealousy. Her modest abode was on Mrs. Vivian Peacock's property. The Widow Peacock was a grand old dame who had quite an estate that she maintained beautifully with the fortune her late husband had left her. Maggie had lived in the small cottage on her property for a few years. It was nothing like the main house, which was nearly all windows on the back side and filled with unique and very expensive furniture and adornments. In the spring, beautiful flowers and greenery sprouted everywhere. The fall brought rich rust, purple, and golden tapestries from every tree and shrub. At the end of winter, after Mrs. Peacock had her extravagant Christmas decorations removed, the property looked like a naked mannequin waiting to be gussied up again. But the thought of Shelly Pinkowski's aunt's house being treated as if it was an albatross around her neck annoyed Maggie. Such a beautiful place only needed a little tender loving care, and Shelly was ready to toss it aside for peanuts. At least, that was what she'd gathered from the heated exchange she'd overheard that afternoon.

All Maggie had was a small, one-bedroom bungalow that she'd filled with her books and mismatched furniture. It wasn't much. Perhaps she'd never have more than this. The thought wasn't horrible. But she knew if she ever had the means to have a house like the one on Campbell Street, she'd treat it like the fine lady it was. How anyone could be so shallow as to see that place as old and ugly was beyond Maggie's imagination. That was someone who came to the bookstore for the latest bestseller and not to peruse the classics. Maggie would never understand that kind of person.

As she went to unlock her door, a shrill voice came from behind her, making her jump.

"Maggie! Maggie! Don't open that door!" Mrs.

Peacock shouted as she bustled down the sidewalk. She obviously hadn't come from the back of the main house.

"Mrs. Peacock, what's the matter?" Maggie went to her landlady with eyes wide.

"Oh, the most horrible thing. Let me catch my breath," Mrs. Peacock said as she flung her long cashmere scarf elegantly across the front of her camelhair coat and over her shoulder. A rich-brown fur hat covered the top of her head, reminding Maggie of the Royal Guard around Buckingham Palace.

"Are you all right?"

"No. Oh, when Mrs. Donovan hears about this, there is no telling what she'll do," Mrs. Peacock huffed. Finally, she took a long deep breath and blurted out her trouble. "We have bedbugs."

"What?"

"I know. It's a horrible tragedy. I'm just beside myself. Do you know how much it is going to cost to have the entire premises treated? How I'll pay for this, I have no idea. I'm on such a fixed income that this is really going to hurt," Mrs. Peacock fussed.

"If you have them at the main house, that doesn't mean I do. No one has been to my house in months," Maggie said, knowing it had been longer than that.

"That doesn't matter. Those vile creatures can jump and cling to a surface like a spider monkey on a branch. Their lifespan is also unnecessarily long. You could have picked one up just walking along the sidewalk. In fact, who knows? Maybe one came in on one of those old books you are so fond of. Oh, I just can't believe it. Bedbugs!" Mrs. Peacock gasped as if she'd been told she had terminal cancer.

Maggie wrinkled her nose, knowing full well she hadn't brought in any bedbugs from work or any other place. "Well, what am I supposed to do about it?" Maggie asked.

"You must leave the cottage for the next couple of days while I have the exterminators come. It's a long process for them to rid a house of these creatures. You'll have to find other accommodations," Mrs. Peacock said as if the whole thing was nothing more than changing a sheet on a bed.

"What?"

"I'm going to stay at the Rochester in Mason City. Thank goodness they had a suite available. The price is outlandish, and I'm not sure how I'll ever manage, but I guess I have no choice," Mrs. Peacock said. "Would you like me to see if they have a room for you, dear?"

"At the Rochester? I can't even afford to sit in the lobby," Maggie muttered.

"My goodness, it isn't that expensive. I'm on a fixed income, and I can afford it. I'll leave you to fend for yourself, then. I'm sure you've got plenty of friends who would allow you to stay with them for a few days. People your age are always looking for company."

"I'll need to get some clothes." Maggie wrinkled her nose and jingled her keys.

Mrs. Peacock shouted, "No!" and nearly threw herself in front of the door, as if a grenade was about to go off.

"Didn't you hear what I said? We might have *bedbugs*. If you go in there now and grab some clothing, you don't know how many of those things might catch a ride on your suitcase or worse… on your person. No. I'm afraid you'll have to buy yourself some new clothes. Going inside is out of the question." Mrs. Peacock stood there with her arms wrapped around herself, her chin raised, and her face stern.

Maggie stared at Mrs. Peacock, who finally squinted down at her watch as if she could read it in the pale light of Maggie's front porch.

"Buy new clothes?"

"I know it's a terrible burden, dear. I certainly wouldn't be asking this of you if it weren't serious. But those creepy-crawlies live in clothes and mattresses, and the thought of it getting out that we have bedbugs will be the icing on the cake for Mrs. Donovan. She will never let me live it down. The woman had lice not nine years ago. This would be just the thing for her to lord over me."

"You still remember that she had lice *nine years ago*?" Maggie muttered and shook her head as the words just came out.

But Mrs. Peacock was barely paying any attention. "I must be going. The hotel is expecting me to check in soon, and I don't want to be late. Remember, do not go inside. I'll stop by the bookstore and let you know when the coast is clear," Mrs. Peacock said. Then she disappeared as quickly as she'd arrived.

Maggie stood there and looked around. Her breath came out in steady streams of steam as the temperature began to drop. Where was she going to stay? What was she going to wear? This was a horrible turn of events. But as she did in most emergencies, she thought of the only place that really brought her any comfort. The bookstore.

As she got into her car, her chest seized up with nerves. "You can't go there, Maggie Bell. You'd have to explain to Joshua that you have bedbugs, and then he'd freak out. My gosh. This all feels more familiar than I care to admit. The bookstore is out of the question," she said, putting the car in drive and heading down the street. The thought of going to Mrs. Donovan's and innocently asking for some diatomaceous earth crossed her mind.

"Oh, why do I need that unheard-of rare powdered sedimentary rock? It is a natural remedy for bedbugs. Mrs. Peacock thinks she's got an infestation." Maggie would have loved to see the look on Mrs. Donovan's face before she dashed for the phone to make a few calls. But, of course, she'd never do that to Mrs. Peacock, no matter how inconvenient and unreasonable her landlord seemed at the moment.

Just as she was about to bite the bullet and stop at a motel off the interstate, she saw a sign and clicked her tongue. "Now, why didn't I think of this first?"

The hand-painted sign for the Old English Bed-

and-Breakfast was lit by a soft light but stood out like a shining beacon to Maggie. Alexander Whitfield's dear friend, Mrs. Burnside, owned the place. It was named after her beloved French bulldog, Old English.

Maggie pulled in and whispered a quick prayer that there was just one room left. The parking lot looked full, but that didn't deter her. With her whole face covered in hood and scarf, she parked her car, jumped out, and hurried through the front door. She made a beeline for the front desk and tried not to look at anyone lingering in the lobby for fear of running into another one of her classmates. Talking to Shelly had been enough, and now that she was out of her own home with a possible case of bedbugs, the last thing she wanted was to explain why she was staying at the B&B when she still lived in town.

"Why, Margaret Bell." Ms. Burnside spoke as if she was in a library. For that, Maggie was thankful.

"Hello, Ms. Burnside. How are you?"

"I'm doing fine. I'm missing our old friend, but I'm sure you know how that feels," the matron replied, speaking of Alexander Whitfield.

He and she had been friends since Maggie had first started at the bookstore. Maggie had often wondered if they'd shared a romance at some time but had never had any proof or the courage to ask.

"Yes, ma'am, I do."

Edna Burnside was exactly what one might expect from a woman who had built her business around the image of her dog. She had silver hair piled up in a bun on the top of her head. Her high-arched eyebrows were drawn in with a black pencil. Her lips were a deep burgundy. Her wrists jingled with a dozen bangles each. Maggie was sure she had never seen her in anything other than a modest skirt, white blouse, and heels. It was a classic look that never went out of style.

The décor of the Old English B&B, however, was anything but classic. An eclectic arrangement of simple furniture occupied each room. There was nothing too flashy except for the dozens and dozens of paintings, drawings, photographs, and sculptures of French bulldogs that filled every bit of wall space and the tops of every flat surface. The entire place was an homage to Old English, the rare and coveted blue Frenchie, who had been with Ms. Burnside for almost thirteen years.

"What can I help you with?" Ms. Burnside asked.

"I was hoping that you'd have a room available

for a few nights. Maybe the rest of the week. My cottage is having some... work done." Maggie swallowed.

"I have a room for you, Margaret. I hope you don't mind that it is rather small. But it has the loveliest view of the park. You are the only person staying here who would even know how to appreciate that. Like the children in *The Secret Garden*." Ms. Burnside winked.

"Oh, thank you, Ms. Burnside. You don't know how much I appreciate this." Maggie let out a sigh of relief. She didn't care if the room was no bigger than a closet and looked over a gravel pit. So long as she wasn't out in the cold and thirty miles from work, she'd have slept in the lobby if she had been allowed.

"My Old English was always a good judge of character, and he adored you. However, he wasn't so fond of that cat. Tell me, is Poe still guarding the bookstore?" Ms. Burnside tenderly touched a gilded frame holding a picture of a silvery-blue French bulldog puppy wearing a red-and-green sweater and reindeer antlers.

"Yes, ma'am. Poe is still with us and as curious as ever," Maggie replied.

"I never was a cat person," Ms. Burnside purred. "Give me a pushed-in face and a wagging tail anytime. Perhaps that's why I adored Alexander so much. He reminded me of an Old English bulldog."

Maggie chuckled. She had always thought of Mr. Whitfield as more of a bloodhound.

"I've been seeing quite a few faces from the past over the last twenty-four hours," Mrs. Burnside started.

"Yes. My class is having a high school reunion. I ran into Shelly Pinkowski today." Maggie shivered as if she'd bitten into a lemon.

"Oh, I remember that one. A whole group of Pinkowskis, and not a one of them lifted a finger to assist their aunt when she was ailing. I'll bet they'll all be packed to the rafters when the reading of the will takes place." Ms. Burnside pursed her lips. "It figures that Shelly was first in line. She's suffered a bout of addiction, you know."

"Really?" Maggie leaned forward slightly. "Drugs? No. Alcohol. She always drank in high school. I saw it myself."

"On the contrary. Shopping. From what her aunt told me, the girl has over one hundred thousand dollars in credit card debt. She'd never have been able to pay it off if her aunt hadn't died," Mrs. Burnside said as she quickly printed a registration card for Maggie.

"You don't think she…" Maggie motioned with her index finger across her throat.

"Oh, heavens no. Those two liked each other. Out of all the nieces and nephews, Shelly had her aunt wrapped around her finger. Not sure why." Mrs. Burnside rolled her eyes as she continued to speak softly. "Probably because she was a charity case."

Maggie imagined having that heavy load of credit debt and swallowed hard. Shelly certainly hadn't acted as if she was in any trouble. Especially since she was donating everything. There had to have been some stuff of value in that house that she could have sold to pay off her debt.

All this talk of money was making Maggie nervous. "Uhm, how much is the room per night?" She held her breath again.

"Well, I'll give you the family rate," Ms. Burnside replied with a wink.

It wasn't free, but it was a price Maggie could certainly live with. Nothing like the Rochester, but once Maggie had been given the key to a third-floor room at the end of the hallway, she was already feeling at home. Inside with the door locked and the light on, she was actually happy. Ms. Burnside had been right; the room was small. Just enough space for a bed, a desk, a nightstand, and a chair by the window. But when Maggie peeked outside, she saw what Ms. Burnside had been talking about.

Dogwood Grounds was the name of the park. A lot of festivals took place there in the warm months. Many lovely sculptures and statues peppered the landscape. There was a playground for kids. A man-made pond sat almost squarely in the middle. Maggie couldn't see that from her room, but she could see part of the jogging path. Even at this hour with just the ornate lampposts lighting the way and the dropping temperature, she saw what she considered crazy people jogging along.

"Good for them," she muttered as a duo in shorts and stocking caps trotted along the route at a steady pace. For a second, Maggie wondered if she should take up an exercise like running. Perhaps it would be good for her. She knew the benefits of getting the blood pumping, and she did like cheese-burgers, so there was a definite reason to start exercising. Perhaps she'd give it a try. Since she'd never attempted to intentionally break a sweat, the thought invigorated her.

She let the curtain fall back into place and pulled off her winter coat and scarf. The only problem now was that she had nothing to wear to bed. Even with the discounted rate for the room, Maggie was not going to be able to buy any brand-new clothes. She'd have to stop at the thrift store and hope for the best. The worst part about that was that she would be within the radius of the books from Shelly Pinkowski's aunt's house. The decision between *new* old clothes or *new* old books was too much to ponder tonight. Everything would look different in the morning.

That night, Maggie slept in her shirt and socks. When she woke up and looked in the mirror that hung over the desk, she crinkled her face. Everything *did* look different. There was no way she could go to work.

"I look like I slept in my clothes... because I did. This is ridiculous," she muttered as she pulled her pants on. She didn't even have a brush to run through her hair, and her mouth tasted sour and pasty. That was all she needed to convince herself she'd be going to work late. Thankfully, the thrift store opened at eight, the same time as the bookstore. She could be in and out in just a few minutes with a couple things to get her through the next few days. Soon, she could slip back into her own clothes in the comfort of her own home, and no one would be the wiser to the possible bedbug infestation. It seemed like such a seamless plan.

Having gotten up early to beat the crowd, Maggie was shocked to see a small but eager line of people waiting on the sidewalk when she parked her car. There was a sale at Sell It Again Sam. After squeezing her way through the crowded aisles, Maggie was lucky to make it out with two pairs of sweatpants, both a size too big, two sweatshirts, also too big, and one bright-pink sweater with red hearts all over it and pads in the shoulders. She'd had to choose between this pink sweater and one remaining T-shirt that read "I drink beer. What's your superpower?" A pair of gym shoes in her size was too good to pass up, as was one book that had a title she couldn't resist: *The Miscreant Dressmaker of Rodenshire*.

Once Maggie had her new wardrobe, she drove to the nearest gas station to use the bathroom to change clothes, only to find it out of service. The second gas station's loo was occupied for nearly ten minutes, with no sign of becoming free any time soon. By the time she pulled up in front of the bookstore, Maggie was so annoyed that she grabbed her bag of clothes and marched in the front door, yanking off her scarf and coat in the process.

"Are you all right? I was starting to get worried," Joshua asked. He rang up a customer buying the latest romantic best-seller before looking at his watch.

Maggie only huffed as she walked to the back of the store for some privacy to change her clothes.

When she finally emerged, Joshua had to stifle a giggle.

"Don't say a word. I'm not in the mood," Maggie said and began her daily tasks around the shop.

"You look very… comfortable," Joshua needled. "Do you want to talk about it?"

"Nope," she replied. She ducked into the display window and set to work.

The day went by without her even parting her lips to speak to anyone. She was prepared for every one of her classmates to come in today. It was that kind of day. But as miracles always find their way, not a single familiar face showed up.

When quitting time finally came around, Maggie decided there was no better time to try her hand at running. She was already dressed for it. Her nerves were all jittery, and her head was a jumble of thoughts that felt like jigsaw puzzle pieces that didn't fit. She parked in front of the B&B, followed the sidewalk around the lovely three-story home, and found the jogging path. Ahead of her was an empty route with no one to judge or stare. It was perfect. She began to run. And after about fifteen seconds, after her thigh muscles started to burn and her panting became worse than someone who smoked two packs of cowboy killers a day, she decided a *brisk walk* was what she really needed.

Much to her surprise, the path was very well lit. It looked pretty at this time of evening. Ahead of her, others trod the path, some walking and holding hands and some jogging. Never again would she criticize those who chose running for their exercise. It was hard. Still, Maggie thought they were crazy but kind of cool.

Off to her right was a path that, according to the large wooden map of the park, made the trip shorter. Maggie turned, and within seconds, she was alone. She listened and heard the rustling of animals across patches of snow and over dried leaves. A light, warmish breeze made Maggie guess the temp was in the midforties. After a couple of deep breaths, she was feeling better. She had clothes, even if they weren't very stylish. She'd be warm tonight, even if she wasn't in her own bed. In fact, the fresh air and starry night made her not want to go inside her little room too soon. A long walk really was what she wanted.

Chapter 4

*C*omplaining *never changed anything*, Maggie thought as she veered off the beaten path and headed in the direction of Campbell Street. She had to admit that she was comfortable, warm, and dry. Her feet were snug in her new shoes, and her head was clearing with each step.

That was why she had decided to go see the house that Shelly's aunt had owned. She was sure it would be dark and brooding, but it didn't matter. There was something romantic about the place even in the dark of a winter night. Maggie thought the old house deserved an audience before it was sold and the new owners made it some bland, beige monster that looked no different from the houses around it.

This time, she was coming from the opposite direction than when she had been in her car. No U-Haul was parked in front of the driveway. The current For Sale sign stuck in the yard read, By Owner.

A soft glow came from all the windows. Perhaps Shelly was staying there until the place sold. It was a huge house for one person. Maggie decided she would have kept the lights in every room on too. But Maggie shook her head at the way Shelly had talked about the house and its contents. Shelly was probably in the suite next to Mrs. Peacock at the Rochester, enjoying room service and a bathtub so big a person could swim laps in it. The lights had to be on timers or something.

As Maggie strolled past, she could see some of the décor in the house. Empty bookcases that stretched to the ceilings. Some of the windows still had Irish curtains draped across them. One window had a Tiffany lamp in it. Another looked like an old-fashioned storm lamp.

"I'll bet all the floors are hardwood," Maggie muttered. "And crown molding along every door-frame. I wonder."

It didn't take much for Maggie to convince herself there was no harm in walking up and peeking in a couple windows. Besides, it wasn't as if anyone was living there. Everyone in town had to know the previous owner was dead. Maggie probably wouldn't be the first person to do so since the house had gone up for sale. *It is a completely acceptable action to take whether you are considering buying the house or just snooping*, she told herself.

So without hesitation, Maggie walked up the driveway and across the sidewalk to the porch and, on tiptoes, went up the steps. At first, she held her breath and listened for any sounds from inside the house—a television or radio, perhaps. But it was very quiet. In fact, it was an empty and lifeless sort of quiet. Maggie felt a shiver run across her shoulders but shook it off as a result of the temperature dropping. She peeked inside.

To her horror, she saw an outdated, faded, and stained powder-blue shag rug stretching from wall to wall in the living room.

"Why?" Maggie muttered as she put her hand to her throat. The walls that were not covered by bookcases were, instead, covered with wood paneling as far as she could see.

She shook her head in surprise. Maybe Shelly

had been right and this place was full of old, ugly things. *Of course, Shelly is addicted to shopping, so who knows.*

Upon closer inspection of the lamp, Maggie saw that it wasn't an authentic Tiffany but had a dolphin and *Sea World 1988* on the panel of stained glass that faced inward.

"Wow." Maggie stared. Curiosity had her in a death grip, and she had to see into a couple other rooms, even if it meant climbing the trellis twelve feet in the air to peek in.

The room with the storm lamp was more of the same except the carpet was gold and not blue. As she crept around the side of the house, the windows were, unfortunately, too high for her to see through.

But as she made her way around to the back, she was startled to see the coach house door standing wide open and a light shining from inside. Thinking it might be Shelly, Maggie had a sudden urge to inquire a little more about the house and maybe get a quick tour. Squaring her shoulders and putting on her most serious face, she cleared her throat as she approached the open coach house.

"Hello?" she called. "Is anyone home?"

It wouldn't be odd for her to ask about the

property. If Shelly Pinkowski was selling the place on her own, she'd have to expect people to drop in after seeing the sign. Plus, her old classmate had no idea how much money Maggie had or didn't have. It was completely plausible that she'd saved her pennies and had just been waiting for this place to go on the market. That was the story Maggie had concocted, and she was going to stick to it.

As soon as she stepped over the threshold into the building, an odd sense of stillness settled over her. The sound of a dog barking in the distance and the rustling of dried stalks of dead wildflowers nudged by the slight breeze seemed to stop at the door and not venture inside. Maggie took a deep breath. It smelled like an antique shop inside, although as far as Maggie could see, there weren't any vintage treasures within. Some old blankets were stacked neatly in a corner with a couple of brooms and rakes across from them. Half a dozen boxes were filled with things Maggie could see belonged in a coach house entry: gardening tools, terra-cotta pots, shovels, a pair of gardening gloves. A set of stairs to the right led to the living quarters. Maggie walked over, looked up, and wrinkled her nose.

"Hello?" she shouted. "Anyone up there? Hey! The door was wide open down here!"

Still nothing. Not even a shuffle of footsteps. But a faint light was on.

"Who in the world puts a house up for sale and then leaves it open for any weirdo to walk in and make themselves at home?" Maggie called. "Squatters are real, you know."

Although there was nothing stirring, Maggie felt there was no reason she shouldn't walk around. Maybe whoever had left the door open was in the main house for a second.

May as well check out the coach house while I'm here, she thought. Without hesitation, Maggie made enough noise walking up the steps to alert anyone to her coming. Her intention wasn't to frighten them or get herself scared off balance and take a tumble down the stairs.

"Hello?" she called again. "Shelly? Are you up here?"

Maggie gripped the banister at the top of the steps and looked around. The apartment was smaller than it looked from the outside, more like a studio than a loft. She was no carpenter, but Maggie thought it looked as if some walls had been added that didn't match the original structure. She noticed there were outlets in weird places, and the windows had mismatched panes in them.

And there was that body lying on the floor that didn't belong.

In those few seconds, Maggie was sure her heart had stopped beating as her mind hurried to catch up to what she was looking at. It was as if she'd caught the last few minutes of a television show after having fallen asleep halfway through it. She blinked and tried to piece together where she'd missed something. She squinted. Surely, that wasn't a body lying on the floor. It was a pile of clothes or a mannequin or something. The light was playing a trick on her. That had to be it. Still, there it was, lying next to an old wrought-iron bed with a bare box spring and mattress on it.

"Hello?" she said, her own voice suddenly sounding exceptionally loud.

Nothing in the room moved. Maggie's mouth had gone bone dry. It couldn't be a person lying there. It had to be something else. She pulled her courage from the bottoms of her heels and stepped onto the landing. Just that slight elevation gave her a different perspective, and she saw that it was indeed a person on the floor. In fact, it was Shelly Pinkowski.

"Oh my gosh! Shelly!" Maggie gasped and ran to her classmate. She picked up her hand and began patting it before reaching to her cheek and trying to rouse her. But the skin was ice-cold to the touch. There was no life left in her body. As Maggie held her hand for a moment, looking at the face that she'd hated every day in high school, she looked for any signs of what could have happened.

"She must have had a bad ticker. Or maybe some kind of allergic reaction. Maybe the stress or…"

Just then, Maggie saw the bruising around Shelly's neck. She froze. The idea of looking over her shoulder terrified her, but she had to. Would there be someone standing there? Was she still all alone, or was the person who had done Shelly in still there, crouching in a shadow or peeking from behind a door? Maggie's eyes went wide.

Without waiting, she jumped up and ran to the banister. As fast as she could, she darted down the stairs and bolted from the coach house to the sidewalk out front. There wasn't anyone walking around. No cars were easing their way down the street. It felt as if everyone in the town of Fair Haven had somehow disappeared and Maggie was the only one left behind. Maggie and Shelly, lying lifeless in the upstairs studio of her coach house.

It wasn't the best thing to do, but Maggie bolted in the direction of the B&B. Maggie's thought was that she hadn't been alone in the coach house, and the person who had put those marks around Shelly's neck was still there, watching her, waiting to do the same thing to her. She wasn't taking any chances. Maybe it was cowardice, but now was not the time to think about that.

Finally, after running for what felt like blocks but in reality was only one, Maggie pounded on the front door of the only house with a porch light on. Within seconds, a man the size of a grizzly bear answered the door. In the background, Maggie heard the television playing some rerun of a sitcom she knew. The canned laughter not only brought her comfort but snapped her out of the shock she had slipped into.

"Will you call the police?" she blurted.

"What?"

"Uh… there's been an accident at your neighbor's house." She pointed down the street. "Would you please call the police," Maggie asked, her voice low to hide the shaking.

"My neighbors? You mean the Zarownys or the Smiths?"

"I mean down on Campbell Street. Look, would you just call the police?" Maggie pleaded, wrinkling her nose as if she smelled something awful.

"Down on Campbell Street? That's not a neighbor. Why are you at my house? What's going on here?" The man leaned out his door and looked around his porch for any troublemakers. "Are you all right? Are you drunk or on some kind of drugs?"

"Neither!" Maggie gasped.

"I don't believe you. You stay right here. I'm calling the cops," the man said before shutting the door and going back inside.

Maggie could hear him on the phone, demanding a squad car come to the house to remove the drunk lady on his porch.

In no time, flashing red and blue lights appeared at the end of the street. Maggie walked to the edge of the porch and waved.

Just then, the homeowner also reappeared, towering over Maggie by no less than a foot. He pushed past her as the car pulled into the driveway. Before the officer had even put the car in park, the man was barking loudly enough to get some of his neighbors, obviously the Zarownys and the Smiths, to come out of their houses to see what all the fuss was about.

"Maggie? Is that you?"

Maggie wasn't sure if the heat she felt rise up her body to her cheeks was because she was relieved or embarrassed. The responding officer was Gary Brookes.

Chapter 5

Maggie rolled her eyes as she listened to the man she had asked call for help tell Gary that he was sure she was drunk and that the only accident she had been involved in probably included a car and a telephone pole.

"Gary, we've got to get to Shelly Pinkowski's house," Maggie sputtered when it was finally her turn to talk.

"Shelly Pinkowski? From high school? She doesn't live here," Gary said, looking at Maggie sideways.

She could tell by his eyes narrowing that he was beginning to think the man who had called 911 might be on to something. "Okay, it's not technically her house. But she's taking care of the estate. Or at least, she was until someone *killed her*," Maggie hissed.

"What are you talking about?" Gary lowered his pad of paper and pencil.

"I went for a jog and…"

"You came all the way out here to go for a jog? It's like twenty minutes from your house," Gary interrupted.

"It's just a skip from the Old English Bed-and-Breakfast," Maggie replied.

"So?" Gary scratched his head.

"I'm staying there," Maggie snapped. She felt bad for a second because Gary had no way of knowing that she'd had to leave her residence for a spell. Nor did he know the reason.

"Why on earth are you staying at Fair Haven's only B&B?"

"Because I have a problem. Well, I don't, Mrs. Peacock does, and she asked me to stay out of the apartment for a couple of days. She's… redoing almost everything. Sort of." Maggie squinted. The last thing she wanted to discuss was the possible bedbug issue. "Can we get back to the issue at hand? Shelly Pinkowski lying in her coach house with bruises around her neck? Is that too much to ask?"

Gary looked down at Maggie. "Are you saying you were in that house, and…"

"Found Shelly, yes." Maggie took a deep breath. "I'm sorry, Gary. This is all just so strange. She was a classmate of ours."

Gary called for backup before turning back to Maggie. "Why don't you tell me how you stumbled on the scene."

Maggie nodded and told Gary how she had decided to snoop around the house.

"I always liked that place, Gary. I was hoping to get a peek inside and see what there was in the way of furniture and architecture. I was actually quite disappointed. It wasn't the elegant, romantic décor I'd have expected in such a regal house. It was more like a staged rummage sale," Maggie said before describing what she had found in the coach house.

Talking to Gary had always been easy. They'd known each other for so long that she didn't think she could ever imagine the town of Fair Haven without him. He'd bulked up since high school and, after becoming a police officer, kept his hair cut short and neat. But sometimes, a couple of strands would fall over his forehead in a curl that Maggie thought was adorable. She told him every step she had taken up until she had bolted from the coach house.

"Why did you run?" Gary asked.

"I had the feeling the person who had done that to Shelly might still be there. It was probably just the heebie-jeebies. I didn't see or hear anyone. Off the record, what do you make of this?" Maggie leaned a little closer.

Another good thing about being such close friends with one of Fair Haven's finest was the little bits of insider info that he'd intentionally let slip.

"I'm not sure. To strangle someone, you've got to get up close and personal. If I had to guess, she knew her attacker. Shelly Pinkowski was not in the habit of making people feel all warm and fuzzy, if I remember right," Gary added.

"Nope. She was not. Plus, I heard through the grapevine she had an addiction. Shopping. Maybe she got in deep with some department store or online outfit, and they came to collect," Maggie whispered as if she'd stepped out of some film noir.

"I doubt it," Gary rolled his eyes.

"I did just see her." Maggie mentioned running into Shelly at the thrift store and that she had mentioned a house in California Wine Country. She also told him about the argument she had witnessed with the Realtor.

Gary wrote everything down.

Two police cars arrived, sirens sounding.

"Okay. Well, I don't think there is any reason for you to stick around," Gary said. "It isn't as if I don't know where to find you if I have to question you again. Just in case there are any discrepancies in your story." He winked.

"I didn't do this." Maggie's eyes went wide.

"You know that, and I know that, but there is an entire reunion going on, and don't be surprised if a couple of people look in your direction." Gary smirked.

"Oh my gosh. I don't like Shelly, but I'm not still carrying a grudge." Maggie shook her head and furrowed her brow before pushing her glasses up on her nose.

"Are you sure?" Gary nudged. "Because I don't think anyone would be surprised if you were. The way she acted toward you was bad, and everyone knew it."

"Enough to kill her over what she said all those years ago?" Maggie gasped then shrugged and looked up at him innocently. She knew he was just teasing, but she had to explain herself. "No. That is no reason to kill her. A pop in the chops? Maybe. But death? No."

Once Gary's colleagues approached him, he told her she could go and to call him if she remembered anything that might be helpful.

She walked back to the B&B, wondering who Shelly had pushed so far to get them to stoop so low. Of course, she was trying to avoid remembering what Gary had alluded to. Didn't everyone have an "incident" during their high school experience that helped define them as adults? Maggie was no different.

Actually, you were totally *different. That was your problem*, her conscience poked.

It was her junior year. Maggie's best friend had been a girl named Sandy Kristman, who was her complete opposite. The last she'd heard, Sandy was living in Germany after getting a job there. Sandy had had a figure like Marilyn Monroe, blond hair to match, and an attitude like a bull in a china shop.

"We'll go, make an appearance, and then leave," Sandy insisted.

"I don't want to go to a party. You know the people who have parties while their parents are out of town are a complete cliché. Not nearly as exciting as they are portrayed in the movies," Maggie had insisted.

"Come on. Where's your sense of adventure?" Sandy urged.

"I wouldn't call going to Shelly Pinkowski's house to crash a kegger an adventure. I'd call it lame," Maggie replied. She rolled heavy-lidded eyes at Sandy.

"Fine. Five minutes. Come on, Mags. Consider it a study of lower primates during their mating rituals." Sandy chuckled.

Maggie couldn't help it, as she found that comment funny too. It softened her up, and they went to the party. It was a bash. Almost their entire class was in attendance, and that was over one hundred people.

"See, this isn't so bad," Sandy insisted as they wove through the crowd.

"It isn't great. Are we almost done?" Maggie asked as she winced.

"Yeah. You were right. It sounded more fun than it actually is. Let me use the bathroom, and then we can get going," Sandy said.

People always got out of her way, and Maggie held her friend's hand as they dodged through the partiers to the bathroom on the second floor. As

Maggie waited outside the door, she was approached not by Shelly but by Shelly's steady boyfriend.

"Hey, Mags." His name was James Bradford. Maggie didn't really focus on James. He was good-looking, no doubt. They were in the same art class. But he was terrible at drawing, painting, sculpting, all of it. Maggie wasn't Michelangelo, but she was better than James.

"Hi, Jimmy," Maggie replied before looking at her watch.

"I didn't know you were coming tonight," he said and leaned against the wall next to her, folding his arms across his chest.

"Neither did I. But I'm on my way out. I'm just waiting for Sandy." Maggie tugged at the hem of her T-shirt.

"Really? You aren't going to stay?"

Maggie could smell the beer on his breath. Another deterrent. Drinking had never appealed to her, and she had little patience for anyone who found it fun. She wrinkled her nose.

"Nope. I think we'll be meeting up with some bikers or sailors or something later. Can't stay in one place for too long," Maggie said with an expression as serious as a funeral director's.

Jimmy chuckled. "You're funny. You sure you can't stick around? I really liked that drawing you showed in class last week. I wanted to ask you about it," he said. "I'd like to talk with you. Really, I would."

"You better clear it with your ball and chain. Shelly might not like it," Maggie replied, her expression still grim.

Jimmy forced a smile, looked down at his shoes, then nodded. "She is a little bossy. That's why I'm going to break up with her," Jimmy blurted.

When he looked at Maggie, his blue eyes shined, and for a split second, she wondered if he was that drunk or if there had been a few seconds of lucidity in them and he let something slip.

"You are?"

"Yeah. Did you ever want to go on an adventure and have someone immediately tell you it was a stupid idea?" Jimmy asked seriously.

"Yes. I told that exact thing to Sandy when she said she wanted to come here," Maggie stated matter-of-factly.

Jimmy snickered. "You know what I mean. Shelly never wants to do anything different or new. If it doesn't have to do with shopping or jabbering, she's not all that interested. I'm tired of that." He huffed and shook his head.

"Have you told her this? Maybe you should. Maybe she's just waiting for you to suggest something really wild and unorthodox," Maggie encouraged.

If she had to be honest, the last thing she cared about was whether Jimmy and Shelly stayed together. By the look on his face, she was sure he didn't know what the word *unorthodox* meant.

"No. Really?" he asked.

"How should I know? You're the one with her," Maggie said and wrinkled her nose.

Finally, Sandy emerged from the bathroom.

"What took you so long?"

"You can't rush nature," Sandy said. She flipped her hair, linked her arm through Maggie's, and started to walk.

"Thanks, Mags. I'll talk to you in art class!" Jimmy called out.

"Good luck, Jimmy," Maggie replied just as an intoxicated Shelly walked past. It was obvious by the look on her face that she wasn't happy Maggie had been chatting with her beau.

According to the junior-class gossip grapevine, Jimmy had broken up with Shelly at the party in the middle of her living room about an hour after Maggie had left. That ensured the blame was all going to be heaped on Margaret Bell.

Although Jimmy never asked Maggie out *or* asked her anything about her drawings that he'd said were so interesting, there were a few murmurs that Maggie was responsible for the breakup. Whether it was a good thing or a bad thing depended on who was asked, but Jimmy never said he had spoken to Maggie about Shelly, just that they had chatted about art class. His version had him offering one of his broad shoulders for her to lean on since she was obviously out of her element. Maggie didn't care. Or so she said.

"I think you ought to say something," Sandy had insisted in the school cafeteria when Shelly walked past, staring daggers at the two of them.

"What for? Call me crazy, but I don't care that they broke up." Maggie wrinkled her nose.

"I think it's a riot, and I can't help but feel proud you caused it," Sandy continued.

"I didn't cause anything. He wanted to break up with her. Can you blame him?"

Even though Maggie had decided to take the high ground, Shelly hadn't. Soon after the dust of the breakup settled, a springtime ladybug had flown into the high school and flitted mindlessly through the halls until it found Maggie's shoulder to land on. The rumor took off from there.

"Oh my gosh." Shelly rolled her droopy eyes and lifted her pug nose. "Maggie. You've got something on your shirt."

Maggie glanced at the creature before giving it an innocent flick off her shoulder. Only after taking a few steps ahead did she hear Shelly continue jabbering.

"Maggie Bell had a bug crawling on her. I don't know what kind it was, but I'd be careful of getting too close if I were you," Shelly said with wide eyes and a nod.

It was a pathetic comment. Not nearly a battle of words that Maggie would have been able to best her at. But since the teenage mind was usually as sharp as a pebble in a riverbed, the comment stuck, morphed, grew, and shrank to varying degrees, giving Maggie a bad couple of weeks.

She survived. Shelly and Jimmy got back together again, only for Shelly to break up with him shortly thereafter.

Maggie never admitted it to anyone, not even her best friend, Sandy, but she'd been hurt. Mad. Surprised at how easily people had jumped on the bandwagon to hassle her when she'd been practically invisible for three years.

When senior year came around, she came in with a new attitude. She'd never see any of her classmates again. So what did she care what they thought of her now? Most of them talked about leaving Fair Haven, and for that, Maggie was happy to stay put.

But now they'd all come back, and one of them was dead. Murdered. Maggie wondered why she cared. Shelly had still acted like the snobbish and selfish person she'd always been, although she'd seemed to have forgotten the incident with Maggie. Convenient.

Still, as awful as Shelly Pinkowski was, she hadn't deserved to be murdered. Slapped across the face with a cold fish, maybe. But not murdered.

Chapter 6

Once back at the B&B, Maggie heard a ruckus coming from the parlor. She looked to the front desk, and Mrs. Burnside waved her over.

"There is a casual brouhaha that's been organized by some of your classmates. I didn't divulge your attendance at the Old English but thought you might like to join them at your leisure." Mrs. Burnside was so elegant Maggie almost didn't hear what she'd said; she was preoccupied with the older woman's jewelry, hair, makeup, and polished nails.

"What? Oh, uh, classmates. Yeah. No. It's been a busy day. I'm going to my room." Maggie wrinkled her nose and pushed up her glasses before pulling her hood down further over her head.

"Margaret, you really should let people see you. There is so much there," Mrs. Burnside said.

Maggie blushed and nodded but still didn't change her mind. The last thing she wanted was to go in there, sweaty and stunned, only to reveal that she'd found Shelly Pinkowski's body at her dead aunt's house. Nope. It was a hot shower and bed for Margaret Bell.

But as with any small town, news traveled fast, and by the following morning, even the tourists and visitors knew there had been a gruesome death in Fair Haven at the home of one of the town's best-known recluses.

As Maggie ventured out of her room, ready to go to work, she was annoyed to run into one of her classmates, Rich Murphy.

"Wait a minute. Wait, don't tell me." He stood in the hallway and pointed at Maggie. He had had a huge forehead in high school. With his receding hairline, it had gotten even bigger.

She pushed up her glasses and stared at him.

"Margo. That's it. Margo Bell," he said while nodding and rocking from side to side as if he'd just answered the Double Jeopardy question. Little did he know he'd answered wrong. But Maggie didn't bother to correct him.

"Good morning, Rich." Maggie snapped her fingers then pointed at the man. "I gotta get to work. I'm going to be…"

"No. Wait. Not Margo. Maggie. Maggie Bell. That's your name. You were in the art club. I remember now. Sure. You look good." He smiled a dopey grin and kept nodding like those bobbleheads people had in their cars.

"Thanks, Rich. Uhm… you played football, if I remember right. Did you go pro? I don't really watch sports, so I'd have no idea if you did." Maggie's small talk was pitiful.

"Wow. You remembered my name. Cool. No. Didn't go pro. Busted my knee. I sell insurance now. It's not glamorous, but it pays the bills." He continued to nod. "So, you said you are going to work? I'll walk with you. I need to get out for some fresh air. Thinking of going for a run through the park. Say, you going to the reunion?" he asked.

This was the longest conversation she'd ever had with Rich Murphy. He had not been in her small circle of friends at school. His sudden interest in being her escort ruffled her feathers.

"I'm in a hurry and…"

"So, did you hear what happened to Shelly Pinkowski? You remember Shelly, right?" Rich asked with behavior that reminded Maggie of a puppy suddenly introduced to an old dog.

"No," Maggie lied. "What happened?"

"Dead." Rich answered with his chin raised. "Murdered."

"What? How do you know?"

"It's all over town. Everyone was talking about it this morning. Well, everyone here." Rich said and looked up and down the parlor. They were the only ones there at the moment, and Maggie hoped it would stay that way. "Someone ran into Gary Brookes, and he mentioned it. Can you believe that guy became a cop?"

"Yes, I can," Maggie replied.

"I guess I better be nice. He might throw me in jail." Rich guffawed at his own joke.

"If only," Maggie replied before distracting Rich with a question. "So, what did you hear about Shelly?"

Rich looked around, took a deep breath, and slipped his hand through the crook of Maggie's arm to slow her steps. "I heard that she was found in a pool of her own blood, barely recognizable. Beaten and strangled," he said with eyes wide, still nodding.

"What? That's not what happened," Maggie

muttered then cleared her throat. "Who did you get the scoop from?"

"Brian O'Keefe. Remember him?" Rich nodded some more.

"Yeah." Maggie squinted at Rich.

Brian O'Keefe was the only person she could think of who was as daft as Rich Murphy. They had hung around together in high school along with a couple of other guys whom, Maggie was sure, she'd have the misfortune to run into before the week was over.

"Brian said he got this information from Gary."

"Really?" Maggie knew for a fact that Gary would have never divulged such sensitive information to a chucklehead like Brian O'Keefe. Nor would he have exaggerated the facts for him.

"Brian said he'd gone to Shelly's house and Gary was already there." Rich finally let go of Maggie's arm and scratched the back of his neck. "Hey, would you like to go get a cup of coffee or something? Maybe hang out today?"

Maggie's muscles jerked as if she'd suddenly discovered a spider dangerously close to her. "I have to go to work. Sorry."

"Oh, hey. No problem. Yeah, I should get that

run in. I'll see you at the reunion. We can talk more then," Rich said, resuming his nodding.

Maggie hustled out of the B&B before anyone else from her past made an appearance. However, this new information burned in her mind as if she'd left an iron on in her house or was driving with the needle dipping below an eighth of a tank of gas. First of all, she had found Shelly's body, and the woman had not been beaten or lying in a pool of blood. She had been strangled, though. Had Gary told Brian O'Keefe that, or did Brian know because he did it?

For the first time, Maggie was determined to find one of her classmates and confront him *immediately*. Immediately after *work*, that was.

As soon as she walked into the café, Babs squealed, making Maggie clutch at her heart. Babs had been running the café since Joshua first opened it and was pulling in a pretty penny with her sandwiches and soups and bubbly personality. Maggie didn't think Babs ever came to work in a bad mood. No matter how many people she encountered, she was always smiling and quick with a compliment or a bit of sarcasm when the situation called for it. No one could ever call her a dumb blonde.

"Mags! I just love these decorations! They are so

cute. They remind me of when I was in grade school!" Babs shouted as she bagged a couple of heart-shaped cookies for a lady who looked as if she might be buying for some grandkids.

"Glad you like them," Maggie replied awkwardly.

Babs was wearing a tight-fitting pink shirt that had a heart cutout that revealed a glimpse of cleavage. Her blond hair was pulled back in a ponytail with a red scarf holding her bangs in place. She looked as if she had stepped off the set of *Happy Days*.

"You always know the right things to use to decorate this place. I had so much fun putting these things up. You really have a talent. When will you be done with the window in the bookstore? I'm dying to see what you are going to do with it." Babs winked at her customer and nodded toward the bookstore entrance.

"Uhm, I'm not sure. Joshua keeps breathing down my neck, so I suspect sooner rather than later," Maggie replied. She gave a quick grin and wave then ducked into the bookstore through the doorway that joined the two businesses.

Compliments always made her uncomfortable. But it seemed the more she was herself, the more people noticed. The more they noticed, the more pleasantries they wanted to exchange. The more pleasantries they wanted to exchange, the more Maggie was forced to emerge from her introvert's shell. There had been a time when days could go by and the only person Maggie would have exchanged any words with was Mr. Whitfield. They were often philosophical and thoughtful, with a pinch of sarcasm. She had enjoyed every one of their chats. He had been her friend. But now that he was gone, she found herself not just being caught in conversations with other people, some complete strangers, but actually enjoying some of them. She didn't like them all, of course. But she had to admit her run-in with Rich Murphy, although not what she would have wanted before her morning cup of coffee, had been enlightening nonetheless.

The question now was how was she going to find Brian O'Keefe and get him alone to pick his brain? He certainly hadn't had anything to say to her in high school. The last thing she wanted was to come across as some needy woman trying to recapture her youth by acting interested in an old classmate. It sounded like a bad movie on a women's romance television channel. Still, she had to figure something out, because Brian was lying about the scene. Why would he do that? What was he there for?

As the day went on and Maggie dealt with customers while slipping into the window to work on her display, she was in another world. With every quiet moment, she tried to figure out a way to get Brian-boy alone to talk to him.

"Boy? He's not a boy anymore. He's a man, like Rich. Grown up and a little dopey like Rich too." Then it hit her. He must be staying at the B&B as well.

There was a halfway decent chance of running into him if she put herself in a position to be noticed. She looked down at her clothes—her unique and dangerously comfortable sweatpants and sweatshirt—and thought this was not the way she wanted to look. But her curiosity overwhelmed her vanity. Maggie would plant herself in the parlor of the B&B and hope that she'd be able to corner Brian for a few minutes.

Chapter 7

Mrs. Burnside had decorated the parlor of the Old English Bed-and-Breakfast for Valentine's Day. Her dog appeared everywhere in heart-shaped frames, some painted red, some gold, all with the pushed-in face of the little beastie smiling adorably in photo after photo. Red heart accents were perched on every flat surface, and a fire burned in the fireplace, making the walls glow a soft, romantic gold.

When Maggie got there after work, she didn't see or hear a soul. She was sure she'd missed her chance to catch Brian O'Keefe since she had avoided the previous get-together as if all of them had the plague. As she tugged at her sweatshirt hem and wondered what to do next, she heard footsteps and quiet whispers coming up behind her. Part of her didn't want to turn around and see who it was, but how was she going to find Brian if she didn't? With her nose wrinkled and her glasses resting at the tip, she quickly glanced over her shoulder.

"Hey, Maggie." It was Rich Murphy again. He was with another fellow she didn't recognize.

"I'll catch you later," the stranger said.

"Yeah, later, bro," Rich replied, clapping the guy on the back before he gave Maggie a nod and headed out the front door.

"Who was that?" Maggie asked, her nose still wrinkled.

"I don't know. Some dude I was talking to this afternoon. Real sports fan. Cool dude. For sure," Rich said, nodding.

"Oh. Have you seen Brian O'Keefe today?" Maggie asked.

"No. Why?"

Maggie swallowed hard then looked around the parlor. There was an elegant bar on wheels, where she spotted a bottle of Coke. Without asking Rich if he wanted anything, she went and began to pour herself a glass.

"Hey, are you going to add a little rum to that?" Rich asked with a smirk.

"I don't really drink," Maggie replied.

"I'll take a little in mine," he added.

"Make yourself whatever you want," Maggie said and took her glass, leaving the bar unattended.

Rich chuckled and did fix himself a quick drink.

Maggie stood in front of the window, looking outside, wondering if she should go back to Shelly's aunt's house. Maybe she'd find or see something that could help explain what had happened to Shelly. She took a sip of soda then admired the elegant cut-crystal tumbler for a moment.

"That's right." Rich cracked the lovely silence Maggie was enjoying, snapped his fingers, and pointed at her again. "You didn't drink in high school. Yeah, that's right."

"No. Still don't, really," Maggie replied.

"No, I don't really drink that much either. But sometimes, like now, I like a cocktail. You make people a little nervous," he said, lifting his glass to her before taking a sip.

"What? Me? You're off your rocker." Maggie snorted.

"It's true. You have that *attitude*," Rich said, still nodding, with a smirk on his face.

Maggie shrugged. "If you say so."

She took a sip of her soda and looked back out

the window. Somewhere in Fair Haven, Brian O'Keefe was roaming around with a fake story about a dead classmate, and Maggie wanted to know why. Why had he lied? Why had he said that Gary had told him those details?

"You look like you've got something very heavy on your mind. Is everything okay?" Rich asked.

Maggie turned, looked at him, took a deep breath, then squinted. "If I tell you something, can I have your word that you won't say anything to anyone else?" she asked.

"Who am I going to tell?" Rich said. He opened his arms wide and swept them around the empty room, still nodding.

"Good point. Look, Brian O'Keefe kind of exaggerated what happened to Shelly Pinkowski. I know this for a fact," Maggie said then took a sip of her soda.

"How do you know?"

"Because I'm the one who found her," Maggie replied. "I just wanted to get a peek inside her aunt's house. I'd always loved that house. It's romantic and last-century. So nostalgic. But when I got there, the coach house door was standing open. That's where I found her."

"So what happened to her?"

"Well, as far as I could tell, she was strangled. But she wasn't beaten. I called the police, and Gary showed up immediately. Can you tell me why Brian would have exaggerated the details?" Maggie asked.

"No idea."

"That's why I want to talk to him. Do you have any idea where he might have gone off to? Did he say anything to you?"

Rich shook his head.

Maggie set her glass down and marched out of the parlor.

"Hey, where are you going?" Rich called then followed her.

"I can't just sit around. Fair Haven isn't that big. Maybe I'll get lucky," she said as she made her way to the stairs and the hallway toward her room.

"You shouldn't go out there alone," Rich said.

"What? I live here. I'm perfectly capable of taking care of myself." Maggie huffed.

"Okay, I'll go with you. Just wait here," he said before dashing off.

Maggie stood there in shock for a moment but then realized now was her only chance to make a break for it. With her coat flapping and her scarf thrown comically over her head, she hurried toward the front door, only to be stopped in her tracks by

Rich calling her name. He was pulling his jacket on as if he was narrowly escaping a fire.

"Okay. Let's go," he gasped, a little out of breath.

Maggie sighed, yanked the door open, and stepped outside. *Maybe if you walk fast and just don't say anything, he'll get bored and leave*, Maggie thought as Rich talked and talked about his first wife then his second wife and how his girlfriend had just left him.

"You've already been married twice?" Maggie wrinkled her nose before peeking into the window of a coffee shop and searching for a mug that might be Brian O'Keefe's.

"I never thought of it that way. But yeah," Rich chuckled. "So, how about you? Married? Engaged? Seeing anyone?"

"No" was all Maggie said.

This was a ridiculous conversation that was making her more and more uncomfortable. First, she didn't need Rich tagging along with her as she did her snooping. Second, she hadn't liked the guy in high school. What did he think had changed? Even her sharp one-word replies didn't deter him. He continued talking about this and that.

"That's why I think they should make a comic book series out of some of these Fantasy Football leagues, see? You've got all the components of a real battle of wills and…"

"Wait. Shhh. Is that him?" Maggie asked as she pointed into a barber shop.

"Well, I'll be a monkey's uncle." Rich huffed.

Maggie nodded in agreement that yes, he could be a monkey's uncle. She didn't say anything out loud, though.

"It would look really suspicious if I went in there," Maggie said. "You do it."

"What?"

"If it were a salon, I could go in and get my bangs trimmed or something. But it's a barber shop, with the pole and everything. You go. Just chitchat about Shelly and see what he says." Maggie gave Rich a push.

"You're going to owe me for this," he said before walking up to the door.

"Whatever," Maggie replied and shooed him along.

A jingle of bells over the door indicated he'd stepped inside. Maggie tried to listen but only heard Rich say a loud hello and Brian do the same. As she peered in from the edge of the window, careful not to get caught, she tried to make out what they were saying. Lip reading wasn't her forte. But she could tell they were chatting nicely.

Who are you kidding? Rich Murphy is probably rattling off his Fantasy Football comic book idea, and Brian is eating it up with a spoon, she thought. Still, it was better than nothing.

She paced out of view of the window, letting the men bond, and waited. A few people walked along the sidewalk. Maggie pulled her hood up and tucked her chin into her scarf even though she wasn't that cold. It provided her with enough cover that no one should recognize her.

But at that moment, she saw the Realtor who had been with Shelly come stumbling out of a bar. It was rather early for a bender, Maggie thought. Then she saw someone come out with her. It was a man who was wearing a long tan coat and earmuffs. He seemed a little tipsy too.

She didn't know why, but she decided to follow them. Rich would be okay, if he even remembered why he was in the barber shop in the first place. Casually, she fell into step behind them, careful to stay far enough away that they wouldn't suspect a tail but close enough to hear their voices.

"I don't think it's a good idea," the real estate agent said.

"Oh, come on. It isn't like there is anyone there. And you still have the key, right?" the man said.

Maggie tried to get a look at his face, but she would have had to give away her position to do so.

"I'm sorry. I could lose my license. Besides, don't you think it would be creepy? Not only did her aunt die in that house, but Shelly was murdered. It's too much for me. It was difficult enough for me to deal with Shelly when she was alive. There's no telling what she's capable of now that she's dead," the Realtor said.

Maggie squinted and listened harder.

"You don't believe in ghosts, do you?" the man asked.

"I don't know. As a Realtor, I've found that some places give off some very strange vibes. That's all I'll say. Oh, wait a second." The Realtor stopped. She walked over to the building and put her hand against the brick. "I'm not feeling all that well."

"What's wrong?" the man asked.

"I think I had one too many. What was that last shot I had?" she muttered.

"A kamikaze," he replied. "It's just vodka, triple sec, and a little lime juice."

"Oh gosh. I think I'm in trouble. I gotta… I

gotta…" The Realtor shuffled clumsily to the alley, and Maggie could hear her ridding her stomach of the vodka, triple sec, and lime juice plus anything else she'd had for dinner and maybe even lunch. People on the other side of the street could hear her. Maybe even a couple of cars driving by could pick up the sound.

Before anyone saw her, Maggie ducked into a doorway and waited. The episode seemed to go on forever.

"I need to get home," the woman said.

"Of course. My car is just up ahead," the man suggested.

Maggie listened as she pressed herself into the darkest corner of the doorframe.

"No. I'll take a cab," the woman replied.

"I insist. It's the least I can do," the man pressed.

"No. I'll get a cab."

"You're being ridiculous. What do you think I'm going to do? Kidnap you?"

Maggie's heart leapt to her throat. She wasn't sure what was going on here, but she'd heard about people spiking others' drinks in order to rob them or worse.

"Of course not. But I'm not taking any

chances," the Realtor slurred. She nearly threw herself into traffic to flag down a yellow cab.

Fair Haven wasn't a booming metropolis, but it did have some of the minor conveniences of the big cities, like taxis. At the moment, Maggie was thankful for that. She watched from her hiding place as the Realtor flopped into the cab and sped off. The urge to lean out of the shadows in order to get a glimpse of the mystery man was almost too much. But once she heard his footsteps coming in her direction, she pressed against the wall and held her breath.

With her hood still pulled down low and her scarf across her mouth, she watched the man in the tan coat and earmuffs walk past. He didn't seem to be in any kind of hurry, but as he walked, he mumbled. The way his evening had turned out wasn't the way he'd planned. He wanted to go to Shelly's house. Why? Who was he?

Maggie listened as his footsteps echoed down the quiet street. There were some people across the street. A couple holding hands walked past her, seeing nothing but a dark doorway, not the bookworm hiding in it. A few cars zoomed past. Finally, Maggie emerged and headed back to the B&B. She had more questions now than she'd had before. Not only had she gotten nowhere with Rich Murphy as her sidekick, but she had encountered a mystery man with the Realtor who wanted to go to the house where two people had died.

Maggie wasn't in the market for a house, so approaching the Realtor outright was out of the question. But the woman had mentioned her experiences with spooky things at some of the properties she'd sold. Maggie had read dozens of books on such subjects and maybe, just maybe, could use it to her advantage.

Chapter 8

Galloway Realty was owned by Jude and Joan Galloway. They had a small building located between a car wash and a car mechanic's shop. Maggie had rehearsed in her head a dozen conversation starters to explain why she was stopping by. She was looking for a house for her father who was actually living happily abroad. Or she was scouting out locations for an independent movie she was making. A documentary on houses of a certain time period, whatever time period the house on Campbell Street was. Or perhaps she'd just go all in and say she was looking for herself. After all, not only had the owner died of old age in that house, but there had been a murder there too. Who in their right mind would want to live there with all that bad mojo?

"I would," Maggie muttered as she walked through the door. When the door opened, a high-pitched electric ping went off.

"Be right there," a male voice said from somewhere in the back of the office.

Maggie looked around. A huge corkboard on one wall displayed pictures of houses from all over Fair Haven and the neighboring counties stamped with bright-red letters that read FOR SALE or FORECLOSURE. On another huge board were more pictures of houses that all had the word SOLD stamped across them. The office was not cozy but cramped, with only two desks in it. Both were buried under stacks of folders. The desks reminded her of those from grade school, when the teachers sat behind huge metal behemoths designed to withstand a nuclear attack.

"Hello." The man who emerged from the back room was thin and tall and was wiping his hands on a dish towel. "I was just straightening up in our kitchenette. How are you today?" He looked sweaty and nervous, as if Maggie had interrupted an important routine. His forced smile and squinty eyes made him look sickly. Something was wrong with this guy.

"Fine," Maggie replied, her heart thudding. All the scenarios that she'd developed melted away into nervous, choppy thoughts. "Are you Mr. Galloway? I wanted to ask about a house for sale."

That was good. Just make it short and sweet. You don't need to explain yourself to this guy. All he needs to know is which house. Her thoughts were bold and brave. Her hot, sweaty palms told a different story, but he had yet to extend his hand to shake.

"Oh, I see. Yes, I am Jude Galloway. My wife handles most of the details for the houses for sale. I usually just do the final paperwork," Mr. Galloway replied before scowling as if he'd hated saying those words.

Jude and Joan? Sounds like a Learn-to-Read duo in some corny children's books from the 1960s, Maggie thought before opening her mouth. "I was hoping to get some information on the house on Campbell Street," Maggie said.

It was as if someone had dropped a stack of dictionaries, making Jude's head snap up at attention. "What house?"

"The house on Campbell Street. It's an old

house. Long front porch. Probably three levels and a basement. A coach house out back. It's…"

"I know the house," Jude snapped. "We aren't the Realtor for that house anymore. We haven't been for a while. Not a long while. You'll have to find out who the Realtor is. I can't help you," he said. He flashed a quick grin before looking down at the paperwork on his desk.

Maggie arched her eyebrows. She was not ready to give up so easily. "I saw your sign in the yard only two days ago," she pushed.

"That may well be, but we are no longer showing that house for the owner," he replied and began to shuffle through some papers.

Maggie wrinkled her nose. "Why?"

"Why what?" He pulled his chair out and took a seat.

"Why aren't you showing the house anymore?" Maggie asked, knowing the reason: Shelly had fired the Realtor in her front yard before she was murdered.

Jude took a deep breath and looked at Maggie. He leaned his elbow on his desk and stretched his neck in Maggie's direction. "I don't feel comfortable talking with you about this. I don't even know who you are. You might be someone looking to get your name in the papers or to start some kind of problem for us," Jude snapped.

Maggie pouted and shook her head. "I'm just looking for some information on a house. I don't care what your personal business is, just your real estate business."

"Really? Is that so?"

Maggie couldn't believe how snarky the conversation had become. She pulled the corners of her lips down while she furrowed her eyebrows. "Yes."

"Fine." Jude snatched a folder from the pile on his desk, stood up, and stomped over to the counter then slammed it down like a lawyer on a crime show would do in a courtroom dramatization. "The home has four bedrooms upstairs, two downstairs that could be converted into an office or rec room, two full bathrooms, and one half bath. A new door was supposed to be installed, but the owner died before…"

"Which owner?" Maggie bit her lip after the words had come out. She looked at Jude and lifted her chin defiantly.

"There was only one owner of the home." Jude shook his head.

"No. There the older woman who had passed away and then her niece, Shelly Pinkowski, who inherited it. She was the one selling it, right?" Maggie swallowed as Jude narrowed his eyes at her.

She couldn't understand what was wrong with him. Why was he so snarky? It wasn't as if she was accusing him of anything. But he was acting as suspicious as a cat with a canary feather sticking out of his mouth and the canary cage empty.

Jude cleared his throat and tugged at his collar. "So, you know more about this house than you are letting on. What is it you really want?"

"I am just asking about a house for sale," Maggie said. Although her insides were electrified, she was sure she was maintaining her cool as she shifted from one foot to the other and nervously screwed up her face.

"Really? Let me tell you something, young lady. My wife only agreed to sell that house as a favor to Shelly since she knew she was in such dire straits. We didn't expect her to do what she did!" He pressed his index finger into the file before standing straight up as if he'd just made a big, big mistake.

"Dire straits?" Maggie muttered. "Do what she did? What did Shelly do?"

"I don't know what you're *really* up to, but I will say this. My wife had nothing to do with Shelly's cousin or his family. To think we'd sabotage a sale of a home just to cause a delay in the process is downright slander-ous. So before you go spreading any rumors that we aren't good enough to do business with, just know this: we've got a lawyer ready to jump at anyone who might try it. We built this business with our own hands. So you think long and hard before you say anything."

Maggie's mouth hung open for a couple seconds.

Just then, the door opened, and the electronic ping went off. Maggie jumped as she turned to see the woman who had been with Shelly the day of the argument.

"What's going on?" Joan Galloway asked without a hint of friendliness in her voice. Like her husband, she looked as worn out as an old dish towel drooping over a faucet.

"Nothing," Jude stammered.

Joan looked at him and then at Maggie. "Are you sure?"

"This young lady was asking about the house on Campbell Street. I told her we were no longer showing that house," Jude said with a sniff like Barney Fife on *The Andy Griffith Show*.

Joan looked at Maggie with the same creepy fake smile Jude had had.

"There were a lot of problems with that house and the family selling it. We thought it was best to walk away from the partnership and let the home-owner do what they wanted without our representation," Joan replied.

Although the words sounded rehearsed, Maggie just nodded, looked at both of them, then slipped out of the office. She took a few steps down the sidewalk then doubled back around the side of the building. In the gangway between Galloway Real Estate and the Sudsy Carwash, Maggie found a window that led to the kitchenette Jude had been in when she'd first arrived.

"What did you tell her?" Joan scolded. Maggie could hear through the window because the woman was yelling so loudly.

"I didn't tell her anything. Well, at first, I tried to get her to just go away, but when she insisted, I made it clear that we were not doing business with her *or* Pinkowski's cousin."

"Did she mention him?" Joan's voice trembled.

"No, but I was sure they were in cahoots. Why else would she be asking about the house?" Jude whined.

"Oh, this is bad. Why did we ever agree to sell

that house? I had a bad feeling about it from the beginning."

"*We*? It was *you* who said we should. You were the one who insisted there would be a payoff that would end all our problems," Jude continued to whine.

"I thought I was doing the right thing!" Joan snapped.

"How could you think *that* working with *him*? You knew his reputation. And hers for that matter. I don't know how I could have let you talk me into this." Jude shook his head and rubbed the back of his neck.

"If it weren't for you, we wouldn't have these problems," Joan scolded.

Maggie peeked in and saw them standing at opposite sides of the kitchenette. Jude's head was hanging low, and Joan had her hands on her hips.

"No. I'm sorry. You're not to blame. It was me. I did it. You are completely innocent. It's just that… well, I'm scared," Joan said.

"Yeah. I am too," Jude replied. He crossed to his wife and pulled her to him. She wrapped her arms around his waist, and he squeezed her tightly around her shoulders. From there, the conversation was no louder than a whisper as they talked quietly.

Maggie couldn't make out what they were saying. It probably had to do with the murder and how they were going to skip town to Mexico and no one would ever catch them. Or maybe they were deciding what to have for supper.

At that precise moment, a rat scurried through some dirty newspaper at her feet, attracting Maggie's attention.

Maggie gasped, jumped, and teetered into a dumpster that produced a loud *CLONG*. Groping for balance, she reached for a stack of milk cartons filled with junk, but they tipped over, crashing and banging to the ground. Maggie flailed her arms and maneuvered her feet like a drunken ballerina before freezing in place.

"What was that?" she heard Jude ask.

"Someone is out there!" Joan shouted.

Maggie quickly fled the alley.

Just as she scurried around the corner, all but sprinting and looking over her shoulder to make sure no one was following her, she collided with what felt like a soft but immovable wall.

Chapter 9

"Whoa. You better slow down," the man said.

Maggie looked up. He looked like he'd just stepped off the set of some New York City legal thriller. He was handsome and wore round-rimmed glasses that he pushed up on the bridge of his nose. It was like a yawn—contagious. Maggie instinctively did the same thing.

"I'm sorry," she replied, shaking her head before attempting to step around him and continue on her way.

"Your boyfriend is very lucky you'd be willing to plow through traffic to meet him," he replied. "Very lucky indeed."

Maggie stopped. Her shoulders drooped, her

head tilted to the right, and she slowly turned around.

"If that line really works, there are some really dumb women in the world."

Without another word, she hurried back to the Old English B&B. Her mind had been preoccupied with the conversation between the Galloways, and all she wanted to do was get to her room and call Gary. He'd be so happy with this little bit of information. It was small, but if he would just turn the screws on them, he'd be sure to get a confession for the murder of Shelly Pinkowski. Maggie was convinced Jude was the weak link and would probably crack as soon as the cuffs were slapped on him.

As it turned out, she didn't need to call Gary. He was already there in the parlor, out of uniform in a pair of jeans and holding a cocktail.

"Mags! Where have you been?" he called.

"Doing your job, apparently," she muttered under her breath. Then she saw the other guys behind him. Rich Murphy and Brian O'Keefe were among the group. Ugh. Classmates.

"I ran into Rich and Brian in town. We've been looking for you," he said.

Maggie was sure that wasn't his first drink. "For me? You've been looking for me? Why?"

"Mags," Rich interrupted, "we found Brian. And he's got a totally good reason why he exaggerated the facts of what happened to Shelly."

"Maggie Bell? No!" Brian O'Keefe said. "This woman is hot. Maggie Bell was a short little girl with a stack of books in her hands."

"Hey, hey. Don't be rude. Maggie is a lady," Gary said. "Come on, Mags. Have a drink with us and tell us what you've been up to. I mean, I already know, but you can tell us why you are here at the Old English and not at your cottage."

Maggie's face turned red, and she shook her head. "No. I'm pretty tired, and I think maybe…"

"Nonsense. You come on over here and have a seat with us. There will be a couple more people coming and…" Rich said.

He was rather pushy as he slipped his arm under Maggie's and began to pull her. Maggie looked up at Gary.

"Hold on, Rich," he said, his eyes sharpening.

"Just a second, Rich. I have to talk to Gary for a minute first," she said before grabbing Gary by the hand and pulling him to a quiet corner. The only one who could hear their conversation was the framed photo of Old English, who was looking off into the distance with a look of quiet dignity on his pushed-in face.

"What is it, Mags?"

She wasted no time. "I know who killed Shelly. It was the Galloways."

Within thirty seconds, she'd relayed what had happened, what she'd heard, and how narrowly she'd escaped with her life. Well, maybe it hadn't been quite that dramatic, but she had skedaddled in a hurry.

"Maggie, you heard part of a conversation. I don't know if that is really enough for me to bring them down to the station," Gary replied.

"But they admitted they'd done *it*. What else could *it* be?" she insisted. "I'm telling you right now, they had a motive. They admitted to it."

"What was the motive?"

"I don't know. That's where you come in. Just go rattle Jude Galloway's cage. He'll cough up the goods, Gary. I'm sure of it," Maggie urged, clamping on to Gary's wrist.

"Maggie, the Galloways have been in Fair Haven for how many years? If they did do this, I can promise they aren't going to be leaving tonight. They'd have left already," he replied coolly. "Hey, here's a mystery you can help solve. What are you doing here? I'm still waiting for the answer."

Maggie took a deep breath. It wasn't right that her dilemma take precedence over Shelly Pinkowski's death, but it did at the moment. "Mrs. Peacock insists we have bedbugs. She practically chased me out of my home with a broom. I don't even have my clothes."

"You're kidding." Gary blinked, his eyes kind and understanding.

"I couldn't afford anyplace else. Mrs. Burnside made room for me and…" She took a deep breath. "I didn't know all of our high school was going to be staying here, or I would have slept in my car."

"Maggie, if only you saw what everyone else sees." Gary smiled when he looked at her, and for a moment, their eyes locked.

"Hey, Brookes! Are you getting engaged or what?" Rich called, making the other guys start laughing.

"Come on. Have a Coke with us," Gary insisted.

"I don't know. You guys look like you are about to call a meeting of the He-Man Woman Haters Club." Maggie chuckled.

"What is that?" Gary asked.

"*The Little Rascals*? The television show? Spanky and Alfalfa and the other boys had a clubhouse and called themselves the He-Man Woman Haters Club. Everybody knows that," Maggie replied.

Gary tilted his head but said nothing.

"All right. I'm going to my room," she said.

"Wait," Gary said. He smiled at the guys and raised his glass as if he was a little on the tipsy side. "Rich mentioned that Brian had a perfectly good reason for embellishing his story. What's that all about?"

"Why, you dirty dog. You aren't lit. I was going to be sorely disappointed in you if you were. You know that, don't you?" she said with a hand on her hip.

"Yeah. Now tell me what you know about Brian O'Keefe."

Maggie explained to Gary what Rich had told her: that Shelly's body had been badly beaten when she and Gary knew for a fact it hadn't been. Whoever had killed her had wanted to do it with as little mess as possible. Strangulation had really been the only option.

"We had tried to tail Brian," Maggie said. "Rich found him at a barber shop and went in. But the guy was in there for so long that I figured they were swapping recipes or talking batting averages or whatever. If you haven't noticed, Rich Murphy isn't really any smarter than he was in high school."

"No, but he's taken to you," Gary said as if he was ordering spaghetti off a menu.

"What?" Maggie frowned as if Gary had told her they were all going to be eating worms shortly. "You're off your rocker, Gary Brookes. I think you might have had a mickey slipped into your drink."

"Not quite. I'm drinking Diet Coke with a splash of seltzer. Looks like whiskey, doesn't it?" His sly grin made Maggie chuckle again.

"So? What do we do now? Rich blabbed that Brian has a perfectly good reason he exaggerated the story. What is it?"

"I haven't heard yet. We were just about to get into it when you arrived." Gary took a sip of his fake drink.

"So it's my fault we don't know?"

"Yup. You owe me." Gary slipped his hand around Maggie's waist and led her back to the pack.

She hated to say it, but she sort of liked how his hand felt, although her body went as rigid as an oak tree branch in December.

"So, Brian. How did you find out about Shelly so quickly?" Maggie asked.

Gary went to the little bar and pretended to pour himself another drink.

"You see, on all those crime shows, the cops never let out the real information. They change it up to throw off the crazies who call, trying to take credit for a crime they didn't commit. I mean, what kind of a person wants to confess to murders they didn't commit? It doesn't make any sense to me." He shook his head before taking a swig of beer. "So I figured if I gave out the wrong information, I'd be able to narrow the suspect pool down."

Maggie watched as the two men guffawed and chortled. They really were just as dumb as they had been in high school.

"I'm going to my room," Maggie said.

"There is one more thing I need to mention to you," Gary said, walking Maggie to the stairs, out of earshot of the others. "I'm not sure why, but we found a list of names in Shelly's possession after examining her body. In a pocket, she had a list of about six people. Your name was on it. Any idea what that might be about?"

Maggie's mouth fell slightly open. "No. Who else's name was on the list?"

"We're still tracking them down. No one else

from our class was listed," Gary said. "I wouldn't worry too much about it."

"That's easier said than done. My name is on a list found in a murdered woman's pocket? What are the chances?" She widened her eyes and shook her head before shrugging. "I've had enough. I'm going to bed."

"Really? You are going to leave me down here by myself?" Gary whispered desperately as he jerked his thumb in Brian and Rich's direction.

Maggie took a deep breath, smiled, shook her head, and muttered, "Yes."

She slipped out of the parlor unnoticed as Gary rejoined with the group and distracted them with a joke.

Before she could climb the stairs, the front door burst open, and the handsome man she'd bumped into in the street appeared. Maggie gasped again, her expression as if she'd suddenly smelled something awful. He shook his coat as he stepped up to the counter, looking down as he brushed a hand over his head. When he looked up and saw Maggie, he smiled broadly.

"Well, hello again," he said.

Maggie turned without saying a word and went

up the stairs. She heard the man speak to Mrs. Burnside.

"Do I have any messages?" he asked.

Mrs. Burnside, who was always the epitome of class and discretion, responded softly.

"Thank you," he replied.

As if a ghost was closing in behind her, Maggie shot up the stairs two at a time until she reached her floor. She darted clumsily down the hallway as she fished in each pocket for her key. Finally, she found it, opened her door, slipped inside, and slammed the door behind her. The only other sound was the lock clicking into place.

That guy is staying at the B&B? What are the chances? Who is he, and why was he so flirty with me? Maggie mused as she pulled off her coat. *No. He's obviously a weirdo. Seems like this reunion has attracted all of them to Fair Haven.*

Maggie looked out the window into the park. Pushing the handsome stranger out of her mind, she thought about Brian's reasoning for embellishing the details around Shelly's death. It made sense. Sort of. There were always armchair detectives who thought they had come up with a clever solution that the cops had missed.

The Galloways had a motive. At least, it had

sounded as if they did from their heated conversation.

And what was this list that Gary had found with Maggie's name on it? Why would Shelly have her name on something? She'd hated her in high school. They certainly hadn't kept in touch, and when they'd bumped into one another at the thrift store, Shelly hadn't acted as if they were going to become besties any time soon.

Maggie, all you've got is a bunch of loose threads and no way to tie any of them off, she thought. Maybe in the morning, she'd see things differently.

Morning came quickly. So did a new perspective.

Chapter 10

The next day at the bookstore, Maggie revealed her latest window dressing to mixed reviews.

She had taken most of the décor from Alexander's little office, which Joshua rarely used. It was really nothing more than a small cubby on the north side of the bookstore, butting up against the wall that separated the bookstore from the café. It held his small desk, which was still cluttered with some of his personal notes and books—books that were not for sale but well-worn copies of some of his favorites—and his umbrella stand with his umbrellas in it. On the desk were framed black-and-white pictures of places he had loved: the Leaning Tower of Pisa in Italy, Coney Island in New York.

Maggie was glad Joshua had left the small space as it was. She took comfort in it. It was as if Alexander might have been sitting there in spirit, watching as the bookstore bloomed into a successful little business.

Maggie had swiped an old trunk from beside the desk for her display. Inside it was a maroon throw blanket. Both were now in the window, along with a masking-tape outline of a body on the floor. All around were books of true crimes of passion.

It was a macabre yet very romantic scene, with candelabras, mirrors, and a wine carafe with a glass tipped over. Upon closer inspection, one could see the murder weapons included in the game Clue scattered all around. It was beautiful in a gory way.

"Once again, Maggie comes up with the most unique idea for Valentine's Day," Babs said with her hands on her hips. "I love it. And I totally get it. Bravo."

"I don't know about this," Joshua said.

"What is wrong with it?" Maggie asked as she pushed her glasses up on her nose.

"It's a little depressing, don't you think?" he replied.

"I really like it," said Casper, the stock boy.

"How many cupids and pink hearts can you see before feeling like a birthday cake threw up?"

"I still don't know if we should keep it," Joshua muttered. "I will say it is unique, and no one else will have anything quite like it in town. Or in the entire state for that matter."

"You do know that the main consumers of true crime stories are women," Maggie said. "That's a fact. Additionally, romances are read by more people in hospitals, where they are looking for happy endings. One more thing. Not everyone has a sweetheart, and some people might enjoy a love-gone-wrong tale during this super-sappy time of year."

Joshua looked down at Maggie and smirked. "Do I detect a little jealousy in your voice?"

"Yes. Yes, you do," Maggie admitted.

"Hey, you've got that reunion coming up tomor-row," Babs interrupted. "You never know. Some old flame might show up and ignite things."

Maggie swallowed hard. She didn't want to go to her reunion, let alone have anything ignited. She was more interested in finding out who had clipped Shelly Pinkowski and why.

"It does look romantic." Joshua shrugged and thrust his hands into the back pockets of his jeans.

He was wearing work boots, as usual, and a flannel shirt, also as usual. But it didn't matter. He always looked rugged and handsome, and Maggie just pursed her lips. It wasn't as if he'd asked to escort her to her reunion. And even if he did, she knew she'd be nothing but a ball of nerves around him, becoming even more of a wallflower than she had been during those four miserable years in high school.

"The more I study it, the more I like it," Joshua said. "You're right. A good old-fashioned deadly love triangle is just the thing for this time of year. Only you would have thought of it, Maggie. Only you. Casper, will you help me with the lights in the storeroom? We've got some bulbs needing changing."

"Sure," Casper replied, and the two men disappeared into the back of the store.

Maggie felt her cheeks redden and couldn't help but rock back on her heels for a moment as she peeked at Joshua walking away. When he turned and caught her looking at him, she quickly cleared her throat and began to tug at her cuffs before refocusing on her Valentine's display.

"You know, you could have had practically naked mannequins posed as provocatively as any pinup girl, and Joshua would have let you leave it," Babs said.

"I… don't know what you mean," Maggie stuttered.

"You know, Mags, you are so sweet I bet you don't." Babs giggled. "It's a great display. Your best yet. Want a cup of coffee?"

"That would be nice," Maggie said, happy to have the conversation go in a different direction.

She followed her curvy coworker into the café and took a seat at the high table closest to the counter. There, she listened as Babs chatted pleasantly with customers and told her about the romantic night she had planned with her husband.

"This all hinges on if his little sidekick goes to sleep on time." Babs chuckled.

Since she'd had her son, Babs's husband Roy had come into the café almost every day with the little angel strapped to his belly. "He wants to get him a dog. I just don't know about that. We are exhausted enough without a puppy around. Oh, but if it would really make Roy happy, I suppose it isn't too much to ask. He's such a good guy."

"What kind of dog does he want?" Maggie asked as she took a warm cup from Babs filled with strong black coffee.

"A boxer. They are the cutest things. Good around kids. But they get wild when they are excited. Males especially. Of course, that goes without saying, I suppose." Babs and Maggie both chuckled.

Just then, the bells over the café door began to jingle. Maggie turned and peeked over her shoulder only to see the same man whom she'd collided with yesterday and encountered again at the B&B. Her breath hitched in her throat, and her pulse raced as though she'd walked through a spider web.

What is wrong with you? Pull yourself together, her mind scolded. She looked down at her coffee mug, letting her hair fall in a way that she hoped covered her face.

"I'll take a small coffee to go," the man said to Babs.

Maggie continued to look everywhere but in his direction. But it was no use.

"Hello?"

He's not talking to you. Don't look. He's obviously saying that to one of the other patrons. Don't look. Just don't look, her conscience urged. But this guy wasn't content to stay in his lane. Maggie felt a tap on her shoulder and went rigid before turning her head. It was him, all right. His round glasses were at the end of his nose. He wasn't what anyone would call movie-star handsome. But his glasses and the blue sweater under his trench coat gave him a bookwormy kind of look that was hard not to find charming.

"Hi," Maggie replied softly.

"This is the third time we've run into each other. I think fate is trying to tell us something," he said as he extended his hand. "My name is Robert. Robert Hallas. My friends call me Robert."

"Maggie," she said while squinting. "Can I help you?"

"Well, I guess what I want is to join you while I sip my cup of coffee. Would that be all right?"

Maggie looked around and caught a glimpse of Babs, who was looking down at the counter, pretending to wipe the surface with an amused smirk on her lips.

"Actually, I'm on the clock," Maggie said, pointing to the bookshop door while sliding off her stool. "I have to get to work."

"Oh, you work in the bookstore? Well, that's great. I'm looking for a copy of *A Deadly Affair*. I usually read a true crime story during this time of year."

"Really?" Maggie's eyebrows rose. "I have that

one. It's in our window. That's about the man who killed his wife to be with his girlfriend."

"Yeah. But I hate to say that's what lots of true crime stories are about." Robert chuckled.

"Yeah, I guess you are right. If you wait here, I'll get you a copy," Maggie said. She tried not to smile for fear of coming across as desperate.

"Mags, why don't you both take your coffee into the bookshop?" Babs suggested. "It's not that busy today. I'm sure Joshua won't mind."

"Who is Joshua? Your boyfriend?" Robert asked, his eyes twinkling.

"Oh! No! Gosh, no. No. He's my boss. He owns the bookstore. Boyfriend? No," Maggie replied a little too loudly, shaking her head and nearly spilling her coffee down the front of her shirt.

It was only then that she realized she was wearing the same sweatpants from yesterday and the sweatshirt from the day before. At least her feet were comfortable in her new gym shoes. She rolled her eyes and hurried behind the counter to conceal as much of her ensemble as possible.

"Good to know. So, you're staying at the B&B?" Robert asked as he leaned against the counter. He smelled like Irish Spring soap, and his hands looked soft and strong as he ran them over the bookmarks that were on display by the register.

"For the time being. Some work is being done at my cottage. Well, my landlady is having some work done on the property, and the cottage I rent is on her property, so it's getting some work done too. Yes, I'm staying at the B&B," Maggie replied, feeling like she'd just dashed up a flight of stairs.

"Are you part of that class reunion that I've been hearing about?"

"How do you know about that?" Maggie wrinkled her nose.

"My cousin was supposed to go," he said and shook his head before looking out the window. "I used to live here, too, but I moved away after my parents' divorce when I was a kid."

"Who is your cousin?" Maggie asked.

"Her name was Shelly Pinkowski. Maybe you heard. Bad news travels fast in small towns," Robert replied.

"I'm so sorry. I did hear. I don't know what to say except I'm really sorry." Maggie stood there for a few seconds, awkwardly looking around and wishing there was a way she could just run off to the stockroom and hide until Robert left.

"I appreciate that. She'd been helping to sell our

family home here. I'd arranged to come to help start packing things up." Robert stared off for a moment before shaking his head.

"Again, I'm sorry. I know the house you are talking about. I always thought it was beautiful and would have loved to see the inside."

Maggie looked out the storefront window, biting her lower lip. This was more than awkward even for her. What was she supposed to say? She didn't know this guy, but she had known his cousin and had nothing really nice to say about her. Why had this suddenly fallen into her lap? She wasn't a grief counselor. She could barely come up with anything comforting to say other than "I'm sorry," and everyone said that. For a woman who read at least four books a month, Maggie seemed to always find herself at a loss for words.

"Really?" he asked, his eyes devoid of tears.

"Yeah. It's one of those places that looks like it might be hiding a bunch of secrets and stories. Like House of the Seven Gables." Maggie realized she was rambling and again bit her lip.

"Nathaniel Hawthorne is one of my favorites," Robert said.

Maggie blushed as she tried to control the smile that spread across her face. *What poor taste, Margaret.*

The man's cousin just died a gruesome death, and here you are, making googly eyes at him. Where are your manners?

But it was Shelly Pinkowski, and you didn't really like her. So what's the harm in a little flirting? Besides, you aren't doing anything. He's the one trying to be charming. You don't know what *you are doing,* the other side of her brain answered in its own backhanded way, making her wince.

"Yeah. He's great," Maggie uttered. She slouched and briefly hid behind her coffee cup as she took a sip.

"This might sound weird, but if you liked my mother's house so much, I'd be thrilled to give you a tour sometime," Robert said with his eyebrows raised hopefully.

"Really?"

"Sure. I think my mother would have liked to know someone thought so highly of her house. She was old, though. Who knows what we'll find? Maybe buried treasure. From what I heard, the woman kept a lot of junk."

"One man's trash, as the saying goes," Maggie replied.

"You're so right. What time should I pick you up?" he asked, his eyes bright and his smile contagious.

"I think we are both staying at the same B&B, right?"

"Oh, that is right. I forgot. How about we meet in the parlor at seven? We can grab something to eat, too, if you like." Robert spoke softly as he gave Maggie a couple of options for the evening's activities.

She didn't really know why she'd agreed to this. Sure, she wanted to see the inside of that house. Peeking through the windows wasn't really enough to quench her curiosity to see the entire house. But grabbing something to eat? It was starting to sound like a date, and she had no idea how or why that happened.

"Uhm, can we keep it casual?" *My clothes are in my house, and it's being sprayed for bedbugs.* She winced. "It's just that my nice clothes are at the cleaners, and when it's this cold outside, I just bundle up. Fashion takes a back seat." She chortled as she looked at the time on her register.

"Whatever you like. I'm looking forward to it, Maggie. See you at seven," Robert said before leaving.

Just as he was about to step through the door, Gary appeared. His face was serious as he came into the bookstore.

"You look like you've seen a ghost," Maggie observed.

"Not quite. But you aren't going to believe this," Gary said, looking at Robert.

"Oh, uh, Officer Gary Brookes, this is Robert Hallas. Shelly Pinkowski's cousin. He was in town to settle the estate with Shelly when she…" Maggie let the words trail off.

Thankfully, Gary was on his toes and shook Robert's hand. "Nice to meet you," Gary replied.

"You too. Maggie, I'll see you tonight around seven."

Maggie smiled awkwardly and nodded as Robert left, setting off the jingling bells. Or maybe it was the jitters in her chest. She wasn't sure.

"See you tonight?" Gary looked after Robert then to Maggie.

"What won't I believe?" Maggie asked.

"Do you have a date with that guy?"

"I don't know," Maggie replied.

"You don't know if you have a date or not?"

"No. I mean, we are meeting at the B&B, and that's all. He is Shelly's cousin, and I found her body. We're just grabbing a bite to eat."

She shrugged as if meeting a man whose dead relative was the common interest was the foundation of *every* date *ever* made or that *would be made* in the future.

"He's Shelly's cousin, and you found her body. Do you hear yourself? Those sound like the ingredients for a demonic shotgun wedding," Gary replied with his nose wrinkled.

"You said I wasn't going to believe something. What was it? Or have you forgotten already?" Maggie huffed before taking a seat on the stool behind the register.

Poe the cat had been perched on a shelf, watching with darting eyes as people walked past the display window, some stopping to peek inside. He'd decided a closer look at the pedestrians would be better and headbutted Maggie as he slunk along the windowsill. She ran her hand along his smooth coat, down his back, and along his tail.

"I haven't forgotten." Gary leaned on the counter and pulled out his pad and pencil. "It turns out that our friend Brian O'Keefe has had some trouble in the past. Two women filed restraining orders against him for domestic abuse. He's got a hot head, especially when he drinks. And according to their statements, he has blackout episodes."

"So do you think he had something to do with

Shelly's death? What was his motive?" Maggie asked.

"He did have one. They were living not too far from each other in California. I'd learned from her family that they had rekindled their friendship after high school, and it was progressing," Gary said softly so no one else in the bookstore would hear.

"But he gave an exaggerated description of what happened. You don't believe his reason for throwing off the real culprit with false facts?" Maggie rested her chin on her palm with her elbow on the counter.

"Not after hearing about this. According to his previous relationships, Brian would try to choke them when he got angry. One of the women had photos taken, and let's just say we've seen this before," Gary said. "Unfortunately, I can't verify whether he was around at the time of Shelly's death. Not yet."

"You're right. I don't believe it," Maggie muttered. "I mean, I *do* believe it, yet I don't. A murderer in our class. Wow. That creeps me out. Plus, the reunion is soon. Everyone is going to be there. It's going to be like that scene in *Carrie* where she gets a bucket of blood dumped on her before she goes full-scale demonic and kills all of them."

"Yeah. It's just like that." Gary rolled his eyes. "So, where are you and the Cashmere Casanova going?"

Maggie looked up at Gary and saw that he was completely serious. She smirked, as the scent of jealousy was too overpowering to not be noticed.

"Just to a casual place. Nothing fancy. Burgers and fries or something equally simple. Why do you want to know?"

"No reason. He's just a stranger in town. Can't a friend look out for another friend?"

"This isn't the Old West, Gary. I don't need an escort," Maggie replied.

Gary harrumphed, tugged the zipper of his coat up, and gave her a serious side-eye look before leaving the bookstore.

He sure does care about you, her conscience shouted. But Maggie pushed it out of her mind and wondered if she should stop at a real store, not a thrift store, to pick up something nicer to wear.

Chapter 11

Although she didn't want to admit it, Maggie was excited to go out with Robert. There was something that made him stand out. He wasn't as dreamy as Joshua was, but every single woman under the age of forty-five in Fair Haven had her eye on him. Even though there was some kind of spark between her and Gary, Maggie was sure it was only one-sided and that he was more like family than anything else. Besides, Gary was a lawman. To commit to that life took a special kind of woman, and Maggie saw herself as anything but special.

Maybe that was why she was drawn to Robert. He didn't seem to notice that he was so handsome. Like when he walked into the parlor at the B&B.

There were mirrors everywhere, and Maggie had caught a glimpse of herself more than once and fretted over her hair, her glasses, and the snug black jeans she'd bought and paired with a long-sleeved pink turtleneck sweater.

Robert sailed right past the mirrors. "Wow. You look amazing," Robert said as soon as he saw Maggie.

"Thank you." Maggie blushed, pushing her glasses up.

She allowed herself to get lost in the conversation that quickly ignited into a deep discussion of books, authors, and personal reading habits. By the time she realized they were at their destination, a simple burger joint on the outskirts of town, Maggie was smiling nonstop.

Phil's Diner was an average greasy spoon that had earned rave reviews from a number of food critics throughout the country for being one of the East Coast's best-kept secrets. The booths had traditional red cushions that, in many instances, were held together with silver duct tape. The wooden tables had initials carved into the corners and gum dating back to the Carter administration stuck underneath. Music from the 1950s played in the background, and from the dining room, patrons could see the short-order cooks busily flipping burgers while wearing paper hats.

Before Maggie could say anything, Robert was ordering dessert: a slice of homemade apple pie a la mode.

"Whatever you do, don't tell Babs I cheated on her apple pie with Phil's," Maggie joked.

"I promise," Robert replied with a smile as he shaved off a piece with his fork.

"So, you never told me what you do for a living," Maggie inquired.

It was as if the whole evening had passed, and all they had done was discover everything they had in common. Their love of reading was first and foremost.

"Usually, when I tell people, the conversation comes to an end," he said with a smirk.

That just made Maggie more intrigued. "Now I have to know. Let me guess. A lawyer?" she said with her nose wrinkled.

"No. Not that bad." Robert chuckled.

"A journalist?"

"Boy, you are really letting me know who you don't like," Robert continued to tease.

"IRS agent?"

"Ha! No. I'll tell you. I'm the coroner for the

county of Penobscot," he said before helping himself to another bite of pie.

"Really? People stop talking to you because of that? I hate to tell you that I find that fascinating. Does that make me weird?" Maggie whispered.

"Yes. But I mean that as a compliment," Robert replied in an equally hushed voice.

Maggie sat back as Robert took her on an adventure, explaining how he had gotten to this point through a couple of family ties and an interest in mysteries. He'd thought it was just a natural course of events. "But lately, I've had some inklings to try my hand at something new. Public office," he said. He sat back in his chair, watching Maggie's reaction.

"Really?" Maggie crinkled her nose.

"I know, I know. Politicians don't have the greatest reputation. But I think I could really do some good," Robert said almost apologetically.

Maggie took a deep breath and couldn't stop herself from smiling at Robert across the table. "You can't live for other people, or you'll never be happy. I think someone famous said that, but I can't remember who."

"You know, you are the only person to say something like that. Everyone else immediately demands I pick a side and wants to argue. That isn't what I want to do. I don't want to argue. I want to make things better for the people of my county. It's that simple." Robert shrugged.

A hush settled over the table for a few awkward seconds before he spoke again. "If you don't mind my asking, what were you doing at Shelly's place when you… you know," he asked softly.

"I was really hoping to talk to her for a few minutes and see the inside of the house. I know that sounds silly and maybe even a little unbelievable, but it's true. We were never close in high school, yet she had seemed so willing to spill her guts when I ran into her a few days before," Maggie said.

"You ran into her before? Where? What was she doing?" Robert asked.

"She was donating some things to the thrift store. Books. Dishes. Linens. The normal stuff that's gotten rid of first when a house is being emptied," Maggie replied.

Robert's shoulders relaxed, and he sat back in his chair.

"She told me about how she was close with her aunt."

"She was. I'm ashamed to say I never got along that well with my mother. We were just two different people. But I called her once a week to see if she needed anything. It wouldn't have been any kind of hardship to drive down. But she always told me no." Robert grimaced as if the words were clumsy and had tripped out of his mouth.

"It happens," Maggie replied. "I didn't know your mom at all, but I'm sorry for your loss. Both of them." Now it was Maggie's turn to wince at her own words.

"Boy, we sure did bring this good time to a grinding halt." Robert chuckled. "How about I give you the grand tour of my mother's house now?"

"Really? Won't that be hard for you?" Maggie asked, trying to hide her excitement.

Robert had lost two relatives, one being his mother. It wasn't very classy to take such an opportunity to satisfy her own curiosity at a time like this. But he had offered.

He waved the waitress over for the check and, without looking at the total, handed her a hundred-dollar bill. When she brought back the change, he left a twenty on the table and pocketed the rest. He stood and held Maggie's coat open for her. Her heart raced a little when his bare hand brushed against her cheek as he bundled the coat around her as if he was making sure not a wisp of cold air could come through. She smiled and looked down at the floor, feeling her cheeks burn as her glasses slid a little down her nose.

"Shall we?" he asked, offering her his arm.

She linked her hand into the crook of his elbow, and they left Phil's Diner. They resumed their conversation in an easy, casual manner, discussing Maggie's job at the bookstore and her friends there. It was a beautifully warm night for February, with a temperature way over thirty-two degrees. A slight fog floated in the air, giving the streetlamps a heavenly aura while making the street and sidewalk look dreamlike.

It was a perfect night. Maggie was surprised at how much fun she was having. It was as if she had known Robert for a long time, and they'd just picked up where they'd left off at a different time, in a different place where they'd somehow first met.

Once at Campbell Street, Robert parked the car down the block from his mother's house.

"Why are you parking so far away?"

"So I can walk with you and hold your hand for a spell," he replied as if it was the most natural thing in the world.

"You're kidding," she muttered.

"Not at all," he replied. He hopped out of the

car, dashed around the side, and opened her door for her.

Maggie wasn't sure if this was real or not. Part of her wanted desperately to doubt Robert's sincerity, but another part of her thought maybe, just maybe, he was like this. Maybe he was an old-fashioned gentleman type of fellow who knew that treating a girl like men did in the old movies was really what they all secretly wanted. At least, it was what Maggie wanted.

She let him take hold of her hand, and they approached the house. Yellow police tape slashed across the door and along the side of the building, stretching to the coach house.

"Looks like the tour will have to be postponed," Maggie said. She knew her friend, Officer Gary Brookes, had probably strung that tape across the place.

"What are you talking about? Where's your sense of adventure?" Robert whispered as he squeezed her hand.

It wasn't as if she hadn't snuck into places before. She'd been rather bold in some of her adventures around Fair Haven. But this didn't feel right. "No, Robert. We shouldn't. It is a crime scene," she whispered.

"The coach house is. Not the main house. Come on. I know a secret passage. No one will ever know." His smile was wonderfully mischievous, and his eyes twinkled under the streetlight. "Besides, I grew up in this house until I was ten. It's not trespassing if it's your home."

It made perfect sense. Maggie had to admit that she was excited about the prospect of sneaking into the glamorous old house that she'd admired for so many years. Plus, nothing was more inviting than the prospect of a secret passage. What had Robert meant by that?

"Check this out," he said. He took her hand and led her around the back of the house.

Behind a patch of thick, dry vines was a door. All Maggie could think was that it was like something out of a Nancy Drew novel. It was a thick wooden door with an old-fashioned skeleton-key lock and ornate hinges. The paint was severely chipped. The sound of the vines being pushed aside reminded Maggie of snapping dried spaghetti so it would fit in a pot of boiling water.

"Do you have a key?" Maggie whispered.

Robert bounced his eyebrows and grinned. He reached into his pocket and pulled out a long, delicate skeleton key. With a charming click, click, snap, the lock was slipped, and the doorknob turned easily. However, the creaky sound of the rusted hinges and the old, neglected wood made the hairs on Maggie's neck stand up. She looked over her shoulder. The air from the cold February night mingled with the stale air of the house. It reminded Maggie of the books she'd bought from the thrift store. It wasn't a bad smell. On the contrary, it reminded her of an antique shop.

"Ready?" Robert asked.

Maggie was about to step across the threshold when she froze. A thud brought the adventure to a screeching halt—a thud from inside what was supposed to be an empty house.

Chapter 12

"What was that?" Maggie whispered.

"I don't know," Robert replied. He squeezed Maggie's hand and pulled her to him.

"We should go," Maggie hissed. "Call the police. No one is supposed to be here, right?"

"Right. But this is my family's house. No one should be in there but family, and that's me," Robert said, his voice firm. "You go. I'm going to check this out."

"Robert, no. You don't want to go in there alone. What if there is someone in there who is dangerous? Let's call Gary. He'll help." Maggie squeezed his hand.

"Maybe you are right," Robert said.

Just then, a door slammed shut inside the house, making both of them jump.

Carefully but quickly, Robert pulled the door shut. The creek of the wood and snap of the lock seemed to echo through the yard like crashing cymbals. Before anything else could happen, Maggie pulled Robert out from behind the dried vines. She let go of his hand, and they both ran around the side of the house, past the coach house, and down the driveway to the sidewalk and then in the direction of the car.

Once they were far enough from the house, Robert started to chuckle. It was contagious. Maggie started to giggle while catching her breath, making her even more giddy.

"That was crazy," Maggie said through laughs.

"You heard that, right? A door slammed inside the house. Someone is in there," Robert said as he looked over his shoulder.

"Does anyone else have keys? Maybe Shelly gave them to someone and they were doing something inside the house. Harmless. Just collecting some old bills or turning the heat and water off," Maggie offered.

"Really? You think that might be it?" Robert

tittered. "You really don't know much about that house, do you?"

"What else should I know?"

"Have you ever heard of the Winchester house?" Robert asked as they walked back to his car.

"Have I ever heard…? Of course. Mrs. Winchester had construction going on constantly because she thought she had to. She thought she was cursed," Maggie replied.

"Sort of. There were stairways built to nowhere. Hidden closets. Small, secret nooks and crannies. Of course, it's not as extreme as the Winchester house. But I know there are some places she's created that I don't know about. Like I said, my mom and I weren't that close," Robert said.

Maggie watched him swallow hard before she looked away. There were probably a lot of things he wished he could tell his mother. She knew that when Mr. Whitfield had died, she'd suddenly discovered a million things she wanted to tell him. Silly things. Serious things. Ideas. Opinions. It had to be even worse if it was a parent and so many years had been missed.

"I think we should go tell Gary. No one is supposed to be in the house. We can tell him we were just walking past and heard a sound," Maggie suggested.

"Maybe you are right," Robert said after a few moments of thinking quietly as they walked back to his car.

There were very few cars on the road. Even fewer were in the police station parking lot. But one of them was familiar.

Once Maggie and Robert walked through the first glass door then the second, the smell of peaches filled the air. Gloria, the front desk reception-ist-slash-dispatcher, always kept scented candles at her desk. It made the place feel cozy. Even if offi-cers were bringing in criminals from time to time, there was nothing like the smell of a sweet dessert to calm the nerves.

As usual, Gary was behind his desk, looking tired as he sipped from a cup.

"This is a surprise," he said with a smile when he saw Maggie walk through the front glass door. His expression changed when he realized she wasn't alone.

"Hi. We hate to bother you, but there is a prob-lem," Maggie started. She turned to Robert to finish the story.

He was looking around the police station, a

simple structure with a couple of desks behind a wooden guardrail where Gloria usually sat during regular business hours. A small iron-barred cell was in the corner, empty. The chief's office was dark across from the cell. Gary was alone.

"What kind of problem?" Gary asked.

"We were walking past my mother's house. There were noises coming from inside. We think someone was in there, rummaging around," Robert said firmly.

"Your mother's house?" Gary asked.

"The house on Campbell. Where Shelly was found." Maggie swallowed and wrinkled her nose.

Gary looked at her with his eyebrows pulled down before focusing on Robert. "Officer Mike is on patrol. I'll tell him to swing by and check it out," Gary said. "Can I ask what you guys were doing over there?"

"It was my mother's house. We were walking by, and I guess I just wanted to see it," Robert admitted.

It didn't sound at all sinister, and Maggie wondered if Gary was asking in an attempt to find something wrong or suspicious about him.

"It's still a crime scene. No one should be there. I'll ask you guys to steer clear until we finish our investigation," Gary replied as he got up and walked to the electronic board that was used for dispatch. Within seconds, he'd raised Officer Mike, who always worked the night shift, and had him swing by the house to check things out.

"Thanks, Gary," Maggie said.

As she was about to turn and leave, Robert took a step forward with his hands in his coat pockets and timidly inched a little closer to Gary. "Have there been any new developments? My gosh, I sound like some bad television-show cop asking that." He chuckled and shook his head.

"We've got a couple of leads. Nothing I can say formally, but trust me when I say that things are moving along," Gary replied. "There are still some people we are interviewing and witnesses that heard some things. But as I said, nothing concrete yet."

"If there is anything I can help with, please let me know," Robert said.

Gary nodded and assured him he'd keep him informed.

As they were walking away, Maggie looked back at Gary, who gave her an eye roll as if her date didn't meet his standards. At that, Maggie stuck out her tongue and hurried out behind Robert.

"So, what do you want to do now?" Robert asked.

Maggie looked around at the quiet parking lot in front of the police station. The sky had cleared. There wasn't even a dog barking off in the distance. Had there not been an unsolved murder hanging over the town and a possible infestation of bedbugs at her house, Maggie would have thought the town of Fair Haven looked picture-perfect. Maybe it was the fact that Robert had been such a fun date. Maybe it was the fact that they were indeed *on* a date that made the evening special. Either way, she wanted to make sure nothing could ruin it. More precisely, nothing *she* did could ruin it.

"I think I better get back to the B&B and call it a night," Maggie said. "I've got to work tomorrow. And the reunion is still on. I guess I better go since some of my classmates know I'm here. It would be rude not to at least make an appearance."

"Okay. But I'm walking you to your door. I won't take no for an answer," Robert said.

Maggie was flattered, but something stuck in her mind like a small seed or pebble in her shoe. It wasn't a huge distraction, but Robert was just too... perfect.

What's the matter with you? A guy shows up here who

likes to read, likes to talk about books, has a good sense of humor, and you found his dead cousin in his dead mother's coach house. It's a storybook romance if ever there was one, the left side of her brain hissed.

He's distraught and probably still in shock. This isn't a romance; it's a cry for help. This guy probably just needs some serious grief counseling. Not a girlfriend, the right side of her brain scolded.

As she interrupted both sides of her mind arguing with each other, Maggie wondered what Brian O'Keefe and Rich Murphy were doing. She also wondered what the dynamic duo, Jude and Joan Galloway, were up to. But Robert's smile was too cute and kept her distracted all the way back to the Old English B&B. That and who might have been at the house on Campbell.

Chapter 13

When they finally arrived at the B&B, Maggie made an attempt to part ways in the parlor. A scented candle burning pleasantly on the front desk gave off the aroma of sweet vanilla. Mrs. Burnside was probably in bed. There were no guests loitering about, and the soft *tick-tick-tick* of the grandfather clock standing solemnly against the wall was the only real sound. It prompted Maggie to whisper.

"I had a really nice time," she said softly, unable to keep from smiling.

"I did too," Robert said. "I promise next time, we will get to my house and roam around inside. I just know you'll love it."

Maggie blushed as she stuck out her hand to

HARPER LIN

shake. Robert chuckled, took her hand, and raised it to his lips for a soft kiss. Maggie wasn't sure if she wanted to laugh or faint. What kind of guy did that? Was he being sincere, or was he making fun of her? More importantly, why was he being this way? Robert Hallas could have his pick of all the woman in town.

"Good night," Maggie said and turned to walk up the steps.

"I told you I was going to walk you to your door, remember?"

Maggie began climbing the stairs. At her door at the end of the hallway on the third floor, she pulled her key from her pocket.

"This is me," she said and rocked slightly on her heels, unsure of what to expect but hoping nothing would happen to ruin the night. She wanted to thank him for a good time and to tell him she looked forward to doing it again and to seeing the inside of his family home. But she bit her tongue and held it all back, knowing she'd get tongue-tied and stutter her way through it as if she were talking with wood chips in her mouth.

"Have a good night, Maggie." He leaned closer.

"You too," she replied. She turned her back to him and slipped her key into the lock. Every hair on her neck stood up, and she was sure she could feel his breath on her neck. If she were to turn around now, his lips would be right there, and then what? She'd have to kiss him.

Without realizing it, she pulled her shoulders up around her ears and quickly turned the lock. Without looking back, she slipped inside her room and closed the door tightly behind her. It was only after the sound of the lock slipping into place cracked through her room that she realized how rude she must have come across. She held her breath with her back against the door and listened to the muffled sound of his footsteps over the carpet fading down the hallway.

What is the matter with you? That was so rude it wouldn't be a surprise if he never talked to you again. It's not like he's got a touch of Ebola. He was waiting for a kiss. Maybe a kiss on the cheek was all he wanted. Maggie, you act ridiculous sometimes, she chided herself.

Instead of brooding over her childish behavior, Maggie decided to do something she'd never done before. She flipped the door lock, yanked her door open, and walked down the hallway. She had no idea what room Robert was staying in. But Mrs. Burnside always left the register on the front desk. It wouldn't be the first time Maggie had ever snooped for something.

Quietly, she tiptoed downstairs and slipped behind the front desk. As she expected, the shelves and nooks were just as neat and orderly as Mrs. Burnside always was. There on the counter was the register, a thick, impressive-looking tome with gilded pages and a leather cover and the word *Register* imprinted in the fine, dark-brown material.

Just as she was about to peek inside, the sound of voices stopped her. She ducked down behind the counter and held her breath.

"That isn't why I came here," one male voice said.

"I'm telling you that there is more to this than you are saying. Come on, bro. Tell me what you know. It will make the whole thing that much easier," the other male voice retorted.

Maggie nearly choked on the air she slowly tried to breathe. She knew those voices. It was Brian O'Keefe and Rich Murphy.

"I don't know anything. Like I said, I was hoping to fix things, not cause more problems. Dude, there is just so much you don't know about us. I would have never hurt Shelly. Not on purpose." Brian sighed.

"I know that, and you know that," Rich said. "But you saw what I saw. Margaret Bell's name. It came up twice. That's no coincidence."

Maggie froze. Had she really just heard her name mentioned, and in a not-so-friendly tone? Where was her name mentioned twice? Was this regarding what Gary had mentioned to her? That her name was on some kind of list that Shelly had had on her? Part of her wanted to pop up like a jack-in-the-box and demand that these two idiots come clean and tell her what this was all about. But another part of her was afraid that if they knew she had been listening, there would be trouble, and she might end up like Shelly. It wasn't a hard decision for Maggie to stay put.

"I don't know anything about it," Brian said. "Shelly didn't mention anything to me. Besides, Maggie doesn't even seem to be all that interested in what happened to Shelly. You know they didn't like each other in high school. Shelly was so jealous of her it was a joke."

Maggie winced. Shelly Pinkowski jealous of her? That had to be a joke. Did they know she was hiding there? Were they playing a trick on her?

"Shelly told me she was going to find Maggie and talk to her when she got to town," Rich replied.

"I think she was going to tell her about the house. I think she did. And I think all Maggie needs is a little persuading to tell us what we need to know."

Maggie didn't dare peek over the top of the counter.

"Look, I'm not going to do it," Brian said. "This has gone far enough. I don't care anymore. You guys seem to think that there was nothing more to Shelly than that house and what's in it. She was a person. I… I cared about her."

If Brian's way of caring for someone was like Gary had told her, garnering two restraining orders from two different women, Maggie didn't think this show of wishy-washy emotion was enough to convince her that he wasn't somehow involved in Shelly's death. In fact, it moved the bullseye to the middle of his back.

"Yeah. You get very passionate when you care about some dame," Rich said. "I saw the police reports."

"That isn't fair. I've been getting counseling. I'm trying to change," Brian whimpered.

"Yeah, while you were convincing Shelly that you were changing, you could be your old self with Joan Galloway." The sound of Rich's voice made Maggie think he was enjoying what he was saying to Brian. They weren't the great friends they'd appeared to be when Maggie had first seen them.

"Nothing happened with her," Brian hissed. "It was just… a bad decision. But nothing happened. No one got hurt. You're getting on my nerves."

"Look, nothing is going to get done tonight anyway. So long as you steer clear of Robert Hallas and keep this between you and me, we'll be in good shape. Okay?"

"Yeah, Rich. Okay. I'm tired now. I'm going to go to bed."

"You don't want to go out and see what's hanging around on the corners?" Rich asked, chuckling as if he knew it wouldn't take much to convince Brian to change his mind.

"No."

"Come on. It will help you relax to get a little fresh air and a drink," Rich urged.

Maggie didn't care for either man, but she really disliked the way Rich was bullying Brian into going out with him. What was so terrifying about going to the movies, going to dinner, going for a drink alone? Deep inside, she felt herself cheering for Brian to stick to his guns and tell the little twerp to back off.

"Yeah, okay," Brian conceded. His voice was low and sounded tired. He was not the same man who had been such a chatterbox in the parlor the other night.

Maggie shook her head. There was nothing more disappointing than cheering for the underdog and realizing he was not going to make the change. At least, not yet.

The men slipped out the front door, and Rich clapped Brian on the back while leading him outside.

Maggie slowly started to stand up from her hiding place behind the desk and had completely forgotten about why she was even downstairs. With her heart pounding, she looked around, waiting for something to trip her memory.

"Robert. I was down here snooping for Robert's room number," she whispered to herself.

What had come over her? Sure, he was sweet and dreamy and maybe something out of the ordinary and special, but there was something going on that she had to figure out. Especially when her name was being brought up more than she found comfortable. She didn't want anyone to say her name at all. The solitary life was what she enjoyed, and being mentioned in the same sentences as the recently deceased Shelly Pinkowski was unnerving.

Margaret Bell's name. It came up twice. That's no coin-

cidence, Rich had said. What the heck was that all about? And what was Brian doing with Joan Galloway that required they stay away from Robert? None of it made any sense. But Maggie felt there had to be an answer, and she was sure it was inside that house.

But she wasn't going to find it with Robert or Rich or even Gary. She was going to sneak into that house alone and have a look around. The only problem was *when*. With her job and the reunion and still not knowing when she'd be able to get into her own house again, there was so much going on that slipping into the house on Campbell Street was going to be tricky.

"I'll sleep on it," she said. She tiptoed back up to her room, nearly forgetting all about her date with Robert and the way she had darted rudely away from him when it was obvious that he'd wanted to give her a kiss good night. She wrinkled her nose.

"Maybe next time," she muttered as she slipped into her room and locked the door again.

Chapter 14

"Maggie, come here for a second," Joshua said before Maggie had even had a chance to take her coat off. She'd gotten to the bookstore early and was going to try to get ahead of her daily tasks in order to leave a little early and slip over to Campbell Street. But the look on Joshua's face made her frown.

"What is it?"

He took her by her arm and gently tugged her into the cubby that used to be Alexander Whitfield's makeshift office.

"Okay, it's time for you to come clean. What's going on?" Joshua asked.

He put his hands on his hips and shifted from

one boot to the other. He looked so strong and rugged in his blue jeans and flannel shirt. Normally, he had a tool belt around his waist, too, but not today. It didn't detract from his handsomeness at all.

"What? I don't know what you are talking about," Maggie replied and pushed her glasses up on her nose.

"Mags, you've been wearing the same clothes for the past week. You are staying at the B&B. Are you in some kind of financial trouble? You can tell me," Joshua said in a hushed voice.

"No," Maggie snapped and turned to walk away.

But Joshua took hold of her arm. "Oh, no, Bell. You think I don't know when you are telling a fib? You stare right into my eyes and quickly blink three or four times. Look, we have been through enough together to say we are more than just employer and employee. Or am I wrong to assume that?" Joshua asked.

"No. I mean, yeah. But everything is fine. I just don't see the logic in getting dressed up fancy for work when the weather can change at any second. Who wants to be stuck wearing heels in four inches of snow?" Maggie smiled awkwardly.

Joshua squinted and shook his head. "You know

the bookstore wouldn't be as successful as it is without you being here. I rely on you."

It was a nice comment that made Maggie blush and shrug. She didn't know if it was true. She knew she wasn't exactly a cornucopia of warm fuzzies to the customers, but she obviously wasn't scaring them away, either.

"I also have to admit that I like seeing you every day. Maybe a boss isn't supposed to say that to an employee, but it's true. You make work not feel so much like work. But I know that you aren't yourself, and I wish you'd tell me what's going on."

Maggie looked into his eyes and took a deep breath. "Mrs. Peacock thinks she has bedbugs. She made me move out while she has the place fumigated. She wouldn't let me take any clothes, so I had to improvise, and this was the best I could do on such short notice. I'm not hurting for money. I'm just frugal. There is a huge difference," Maggie said before looking down.

"Why didn't you say something?" Joshua asked, putting his hand to his heart.

"Bedbugs, Josh. Bedbugs. It's not something you go blabbing. It's not like a pipe burst or the roof leaks. It's a form of cootie, and you know how people act when they hear certain things, like you have bugs or mold or… *bugs*." Maggie wished she could just slip between the slats of hardwood flooring and disappear.

Joshua smiled and shook his head. "You know, two years before I came to Fair Haven, I had lice." He chuckled. "I'm a grown man, and I came down with a case of lice. I had done some electrical work at a grade school just as there was an outbreak of the little beauties. Half the school was taking time off to get it all under control. So I know how it can be."

"Aw, you poor thing." Maggie chuckled a little.

"People don't judge as harshly as you think they do, Mags. Now, I'm hoping you won't be mad, but I ran into Mrs. Peacock, and she told me what was going on," Joshua said.

"And you let me ramble on?" Maggie pursed her lips and put her hands on her hips.

"Don't you feel better having the truth out there?"

She hated when Joshua was right, so she clicked her tongue and reluctantly nodded. "Yes. But it isn't like there is anything that you can do. I just have to wait until Mrs. Peacock gives me the all clear."

"Right. But I can help a little." Joshua reached behind the small desk and pulled out a duffle bag she'd never seen before. "I know you have that reunion tonight. I've been asked to work on some of the lights they've got installed in the gym. Brace yourself—it's going to be like your high school prom all over again."

"What's this?"

"I told Mrs. Peacock that you had this dance and if she wasn't letting anyone into the houses, you couldn't get to your clothes. She looked like someone had just told her that her Mrs. Donovan had a prettier front yard than she did," Joshua said.

That made Maggie laugh outright. "You didn't." She put her hand over her mouth.

"I most certainly did. The next thing I know, she's knocking on the door last night with a couple bags. She bought you a few outfits but didn't want me to tell you that they were from her," Joshua replied.

Maggie had known Mrs. Peacock for a long time. They'd shared an occasional drama over the years. For all her eccentricities, it could never be said that Mrs. Peacock was ever intentionally mean. Of course, she'd come across as thoughtless and sometimes slightly conceited. But the way most people saw it, she was an old broad who had been robbed early of her wealthy husband and had learned the hard way to take care of herself. That meant never letting anyone know exactly what she had or how much of it. They could guess or assume, but no one knew for sure what Mrs. Peacock was worth except Mrs. Peacock. At this moment, Maggie thought Mrs. Peacock was worth a million dollars.

"Just when I think I should start looking for a new place, that woman does something like this," Maggie muttered and shook her head. "I've got to thank her and…"

"No. You can't. She made me promise not to tell you it was her who bought these. You are supposed to think that I gave them to you," Joshua replied.

"You? Why on earth would you buy me clothes?" Maggie snapped and wrinkled her nose.

"If I knew you needed them, I would have."

"That would have made for a great working environment. My boss buying me clothes like that movie about the streetwalker and the businessman who saves her from her hooking ways. No, thanks."

"It's not an engagement ring. It's clothes to get you through the next couple of days without looking like you plan on sleeping in the bus station."

"Did you look at them?"

"I might have taken a peek," Joshua said, pushing the bag toward Maggie.

"Are there unmentionables in there?"

"What the heck are unmentionables?"

Maggie looked around to make sure no one else was listening in on their conversation before she leaned forward, cupped her hand along the side of her mouth, and whispered the word "*underwear*."

"I… think… so… I don't know." Joshua blushed and shook his head.

"Doesn't that just take the cake!" Maggie huffed.

"Would you calm down!"

"Calm down? How would you feel if I knew what kind of underthings you were wearing? It's an invasion of privacy," Maggie said.

"Then I'll take them back to Mrs. Peacock and tell her you don't want them," Joshua said, snatching the bag from Maggie.

But her viselike grip was too tight. "I didn't say that. Besides, it would hurt her feelings. It isn't her fault that you are nosy," Maggie said as she looked over the tops of her glasses at him.

"I'm not nosy. I was just curious to see if she got you something you'd like. That's all. I couldn't care less what *unmentionables* are in that sack or whether or not you wear them." Joshua put his hands on his hips. "In fact, I wouldn't be surprised if you didn't wear them just for spite."

Maggie gasped, making Joshua chuckle, which infuriated her all the more.

"You really are a thorn in my side. Your father would be shocked, do you hear me? Shocked to know his son was speaking this way. The apples must have not just fallen far from the tree but rolled down a hill," Maggie said as she yanked the bag from Joshua.

Joshua laughed out loud, making Maggie even more annoyed. She tossed the bag behind the counter and took her seat on the stool behind the register. Poe, who had been watching the whole exchange, slunk up to her along the windowsill and gave her a comforting headbutt. Maggie stroked his coat before glaring back at Joshua.

"Maggie, someday, you are going to be sorry for all the mean things you've said to me," he said and stomped through the doorway to the café.

"Doubt it," Maggie replied before picking up a book and opening it to the first page. She was dying to see what was in the bag but didn't dare take a peek and risk Joshua seeing her do it.

What do you care if he sees you looking into the bag? It

isn't as if he picked anything out for you. It's from Mrs. Peacock, her inner voice comforted. Still, her ego wouldn't allow it. She would have to wait until she got back to the B&B. It felt as if today was going to be a long day. But there was one bright spot.

"How did I know I'd find you here?" Robert said after walking into the bookshop around two in the afternoon.

"Where else would I be?" Maggie shrugged and blushed. She had almost forgotten that the previous evening, she had been willing to scam his room number from the register on the front desk and go knock on his door. Thank goodness he had no idea of her pitifully juvenile plans.

"So, you're going to the reunion tonight, right?"

"I'm still thinking about it. I'm not sure," Maggie said. Did she really want to see the people from high school? She hadn't made up her mind. Plus, she hadn't seen the outfit Mrs. Peacock had picked out for her. What if it was ugly—or worse, what if it was beautiful and didn't fit?

"Well, I'm going to be there," Robert said as he leaned on the counter.

"You are?"

"Yeah. A couple of Shelly's old friends threw together a little tribute and asked me if I'd come on her behalf. Her passing has gotten some people really shaken up," he said.

You mean her murder, Maggie thought but didn't dare say.

"I sure would like to have a dance with you. That is, if your dance card isn't already full," Robert replied.

Maggie chuckled.

"Is that a yes?"

"We'll see," she replied and blinked at him over the tops of her glasses.

He smiled and winked at her before standing up straight, turning, and leaving the bookshop.

Of course you are going to the reunion. Why wouldn't you go now? He obviously wants you to. You'd be crazy not to go, her conscience shouted. She watched through the window as Robert walked across the street and down the sidewalk.

She cleared her throat, picked up some books that needed to be shelved, and strolled to the back of the store, unaware that Joshua had watched their whole exchange and had a concerned look on his face.

Chapter 15

Mrs. Peacock had outdone herself. Maggie was determined to buy her a gift to say thank you whether the old broad liked it or not.

In the duffle bag, she found a simple gray skirt and a pink vintage blouse with a wide bow collar that perfectly matched the pink kitten pumps that were also in the bag. Maggie felt as if she had stepped out of a 1950s movie.

Still, as she admired herself in the full-length oval mirror in her room at the B&B, she hadn't decided whether she would go to the reunion. The only thing that stuck in the back of her mind was that Robert was going to be there. But she didn't want to get too involved with him. After all, he had political aspirations in Penobscot County. He had a prestigious job as the coroner, and what could he possibly see in her? She was a bookworm who liked to sit in the corner of any room and observe rather than chitchat. In fact, chitchatting made her feel nauseous. That was another reason she wasn't sure about attending the reunion. How many times was she going to be asked if she was married? If she had any children? What was she doing for a living? Plus, she'd have to hear about all the glamorous, fantastic, exciting lives everyone else was living.

"You don't have to be jealous of anyone, Mags," she said to her reflection. "You are doing all right for yourself. All you need is a good book and a comfy chair, and you are golden."

It was true. She talked herself into making an appearance, even if it was just for one lap around the gym before coming back to her room. She took a deep breath before bundling up in her coat and scarf.

As she pulled her door open, she could hear voices coming from the second floor. A couple of men were talking loudly.

Quietly, she began descending the stairs, walking carefully because she was in heels. They were low heels but heels nonetheless. But she wanted to hear what was going on.

"I don't know what you are talking about," one man said.

"Yes, you do. Don't act like you don't. You know exactly what is going on, and you know I know. You're a phony," the second man said.

Neither man was shouting, but their words dripped with anger.

Maggie made her way carefully down the stairs to the second-floor landing and peeked around the corner. Brian O'Keefe was pointing at Robert. For a second, Maggie thought maybe she should make her presence known, but her gut held her back. Instead, she pressed herself against the wall and stayed out of sight.

"You're a drunk, Brian. No one is going to listen to you," Robert snapped back.

"Oh yeah? Well, we will just have to see about that. Maybe you're right. Maybe you're wrong. Maybe a lot of people will want to listen to me," Brian retorted. His words came out slurred.

Without answering him, Robert stomped down the hallway and past the landing where Maggie had hidden.

What was Brian O'Keefe talking about? What

did he know that no one was going to listen to? Maggie thought there had to be something wrong, but maybe it just boiled down to two alpha males having a tiff. Brian O'Keefe had been popular in high school. From the looks of him, she wasn't sure that his popularity had followed him into adulthood. But guys like him always had a way of eking out an easier-than-normal existence.

As she continued to listen on the landing, she heard Brian mumbling to himself. There were a couple of sniffles as if he might be crying. If he was intoxicated like Robert had said, then it wouldn't be surprising that he was getting weepy at something that had probably happened to his pet duck ten years ago or something just as silly.

The sound of a doorknob being jiggled and a door not cooperating made Maggie peek around the corner, where she observed Brian muttering as he struggled to get the key into the lock of his door. Taking this moment to move, Maggie tiptoed down the landing, leaving Brian to fuss with his door on his own.

On her way to the high school, Maggie wondered if anyone would remember her. A twinge of jitters settled in her chest. Old insecurities started to bubble up. What would she talk about? What if no one talked to her at all?

She shoved away the negative thoughts and squared her shoulders as she approached the front entrance. Red tinsel and cardboard hearts covered the double doors. Inside, the familiar hallway lined with lockers was illuminated by the fluorescent overhead lights. Maggie yanked open the door and stepped inside. She walked down the hallway, fighting off the flashbacks of horrific algebra classes and the absolutely unproductive gym classes.

"Oh my gosh! Maggie Bell?" a female voice called.

Maggie peered over the top of her glasses at a woman behind a banquet table covered in a red-velvet tablecloth.

"Yes?" Maggie replied.

"It's me. Carrie Monnier," the woman said.

Maggie recognized the name immediately but hardly the face. She wasn't the girl Maggie had remembered, who had worn a cheerleader uniform and braces. Before her was an elegant woman in a red sweater with a string of pearls around her collar.

"Carrie," Maggie said.

She hadn't known Carrie all that well and probably wouldn't have immediately recognized her even if she'd walked into the bookstore at noon on a bright, sunny day.

"I'd recognize you anywhere. You always were so unique," Carrie said. She stood up, came around the table, and gave Maggie a friendly hug and handed her a name tag.

They chitchatted for a moment before the inevitable topic popped up. "Did you hear about Shelly Pinkowski?" Carrie asked.

"Yes, I did. Gary Brookes and I still talk almost every day. He was the first to know about it." Maggie didn't think there was anything wrong with that little white lie.

The last thing she wanted was for people to know she had been the one who found the body. Of course, if Rich Murphy was around and the alcohol had loosened his lips, that fact might be all over the place already.

"What a tragedy. You have to wonder what is wrong with people that they'd be so cruel to someone who never did anything to hurt anyone." Carrie shook her head.

Maggie didn't argue with her. It would accomplish nothing to expose the scars that had come from being the brunt of Shelly Pinkowski's insults for several months in high school when the woman had been murdered less than two weeks ago.

"Well, I'm going to go in and have a look around," Maggie said as she pushed her glasses up on her nose.

Carrie gave her a wide smile and promised to catch up with her as the evening went on.

The familiar sound of the bar latch snapping echoed in the hallway as Maggie pushed the heavy gym door open. It was the same old gym, that was for sure. From the ceiling dangled the banners memorializing winning seasons for the track, basketball, football, and wrestling teams. The bleachers were pushed against the walls so round tables could fill the space, and a rubbery tarp covered the hardwood floor. No hard shoes on the court. Maggie rolled her eyes.

But if she was going to be honest, the place looked lovely. White tablecloths were sprinkled with red and silver confetti, and red-rose centerpieces with cupids sticking out of them sat romantically in the middles of the tables. Streamers hung from wires that crisscrossed the ceiling. The DJ, who was set up at a small booth in the corner, held one hand to his ear while dancing by himself to a song of almost that same title.

Just then, Maggie saw the huge portrait of Shelly Pinkowski at the front of the gym. How had she missed it? It was huge, surrounded by flowers and flickering candles. It was almost as if Maggie had forgotten that her classmate had been murdered at all.

"That's terrible, Maggie Bell," she muttered. "Just hope the same doesn't happen to you." She shook her head and walked over to the memorial.

A photo album displayed pictures of Shelly all through high school, her face smug in each one. Maggie looked around and suddenly recognized a group of girls who had been part of Shelly's clique. They rushed to Maggie, who instinctively hunched her shoulders as if she was going to have to defend herself somehow.

"Oh my gosh! Maggie Bell! You look amazing!" Christine Whojik said.

"Maggie! Always such a trendsetter." Debbie Morse smiled with glaring white teeth.

"Gary Brookes said you were going to be here. My gosh, how are you?" Tina Plunk asked before slipping in for a big hug.

Maggie couldn't help but smile. She replied in kind and let the girls from her class chatter on as she nodded and tried to keep up.

"Isn't it just awful about Shelly?" was the conversation everyone was having. Christine nodded. Debbie clicked her tongue. Tina, as per her role in high school, still did most of the talking.

"Yes, it is. What do you guys think happened?" Maggie asked innocently.

It was as if they'd been waiting for someone to ask just that question. Almost simultaneously, the three women took a step closer to Maggie and looked over their shoulders before Tina began to speak.

"I heard that Shelly had decided to give Brian O'Keefe a second chance, and it didn't go as he'd promised," she said with her eyes darting around before finally settling on Maggie's.

"Is that so?" Maggie replied.

"Everyone was telling her that he wasn't going to change. She'd come so far," Christine sighed. "I lived closest to her in California. She'd lost so much money and was divorced, and most of us were sure she'd hit rock bottom."

"Was she an alcoholic?" Maggie asked. These were the most words she'd ever exchanged with any of these girls in her life.

"Yes." Debbie replied. "She drank all the time."

"But she was getting better. She'd joined AA

and had tossed every drop of liquor out of her house. She was attending all the meetings she could. That was where she ran into Brian. I wouldn't be surprised if he had staked out that place just to get to see her," Tina hissed. "He was no good for her."

"What ever happened to Jimmy Bradford? I always thought they were going to end up together," Maggie asked, instantly regretting it.

The way Tina, Christine, and Debbie snapped their eyes to Maggie made it seem as if someone had slapped a ruler across a wooden desktop.

"They broke up the minute after the graduation ceremony," Debbie replied.

"Oh, I hadn't heard." Maggie shrugged.

"From what I hear, he's still single." Christine gave Maggie a wink.

Maggie cringed. "Well, he should be," she blurted.

The three girls stared at her before bursting out laughing.

"You have the greatest sense of humor, Maggie! That's so important in the face of such a tragedy," Tina replied, nodding just as the other two girls did. It reminded Maggie of female versions of Rich Murphy, who Maggie spotted at the bar, tossing back a few.

"Excuse me," Maggie said. "It was nice catching up with you gals. I'm going to grab something to drink."

"I'm not sure if Jimmy's coming tonight, but if we see him, we'll send him your way." Christine smiled happily.

"We're at table six. Come join us when you are done," Debbie insisted.

Maggie smiled, pushed her glasses up on her nose, and wondered what had just happened. Those girls had never had anything to say to her in high school. Now, they were being... nice. So were some other people she brushed past whom she remembered not really speaking to through high school. Could it be that everyone had just grown up? There was no need for cliques and competition since the real world offered more than its share.

As she strolled to the bar, staying clear of Rich Murphy, Maggie noticed a man skulking around the perimeter of the gym. It was Brian O'Keefe, and he looked like he was having some trouble walking in a straight line.

"What can I get you, miss?" the man working the portable bar asked. He was younger than Maggie, with a red clip-on bowtie under his goatee.

"A Shirley Temple, please," Maggie said before

focusing her attention on Brian O'Keefe again. He was inching his way to Shelly's memorial but didn't appear to be in a hurry to chat with any of the other people congregated there.

"One kiddie cocktail coming up," the bartender replied.

Maggie had been so focused on Brian skulking around the gym that she hadn't noticed Robert approaching.

"Oh, uh, yeah. I'm not much of a drinker." Maggie blushed, pushed up her glasses, and then smiled at Robert. He looked dreamy, as if he'd stepped out of some fifties movie in which he was playing the main heartthrob who not only was handsome but could sing as well.

"There are some people here who should follow your lead," Robert said. He looked toward the other end of the bar, where Rich Murphy was loudly yukking it up with several classmates Maggie recognized but didn't want to talk to.

Maggie shrugged.

Just then, the bartender returned with her pink, bubbly drink with a cherry on top. She took a sip more out of nervousness than thirst while she kept one eye on Brian. He had his hands in his pockets and was pacing slowly back and forth.

"So, how are you liking the tribute to Shelly?" Maggie asked. "Everyone seems to be sincerely sorry for your loss."

She didn't expect Robert's response to be blinking his eyes and raising his eyebrows as if he'd just heard a really tall tale.

"Yes. They seem to be," he replied.

"Do you think they feel differently?" Maggie asked.

Robert took a deep breath. "I just wish the whole thing was over. Everywhere I go, people are offering their condolences, telling me how wonderful she was. She had a drinking problem. Did you know that?"

Maggie was surprised at Robert's shift in personality. She took a sip of her drink and said nothing.

"I know. I know. It's a disease. But sometimes, you just have to look at your life and take responsibility. It's up to us to make things happen, and we can't let our past get in the way of that." Robert took another deep breath. He looked down at Maggie.

"I can see your point," she replied softly.

"I'm sorry. I think I'm just suffering a little compassion fatigue." Robert chuckled just as Brian decided to stomp into the middle of the reunion and make his presence known.

"Compassion fatigue?" Maggie asked. The words seemed strange under the circumstances.

"It happens to people who take care of a person for too long and start to feel burned out. I've been tending to my mother as best I could from my home. Shelly's problems didn't just stay in California. I had that burden to carry too. If we are being honest, I'm sick to death of the whole thing."

Maggie wanted to disagree with Robert. But who was she to give her two cents? She hadn't had any experiences like this. The man who had been like her grandfather had passed away simply, without a fuss. She'd never had to tend to anyone.

At the same moment, her attention was being pulled in Brian O'Keefe's direction. He was not doing well.

"It's my fault," Maggie heard him mutter.

"Uh oh. What's Brian doing?" she whispered to Robert.

He'd handled Brian with kid gloves in the hallway at the B&B. Maybe he'd step in again and calm him down. All Maggie knew was that she wasn't going to volunteer. A guy who had been drinking a lot could be dangerous, especially if he'd been drinking as much as Brian O'Keefe had.

"It's my fault!" he shouted, bringing the whole reunion to a halt. "She'd still be here if it wasn't for me! I did it!"

A wave of murmurs rippled through the gym.

"He killed her."

"Did he just admit to murder?"

"Brian murdered Shelly."

"Brian just said he killed Shelly."

Brian didn't seem to care that everyone had stopped and was staring. He turned, and his eyes locked with Maggie's.

"She wanted to talk to you, Mags. She had something to tell you. I'm so sorry. I'll say it for her. I'm so very sorry," Brian blubbered.

Maggie was consumed in a wave of heat that she knew turned her cheeks bright red with embarrassment.

Nervously, she looked around at her classmates. Everyone's eyes bounced from Brian to her and back again as if they were all watching a tennis match.

Brian swayed in front of the overbearing photograph of Shelly. It was propped up on an artist's easel. On a small podium was a book in which people could write a memory, thought, or condolence for Shelly's family. It was like a pictureless yearbook of the morbid. Maggie hadn't signed it.

"Hey, Brian! That's enough," Robert shouted at him.

His booming voice made Maggie jump. Now all eyes were on Robert—and on her, as she was standing next to him. She wanted to shrink into a ball of dust and roll away.

Brian whirled around and pointed at Robert. "You never helped her. You never did anything. She told me all about it. And now you're here looking for it. The proof. I know where it is. You'll never get it. You don't deserve it."

"Come on, Brian. Let's get some fresh air," Robert said from between clenched teeth as he stomped up to the drunken man.

Just then, Gary appeared and approached Brian, holding one hand up to Robert as if to stop him. It didn't. Robert had had enough of Brian's blubbering.

"Bob, I need you to step back." Gary took control immediately. "Brian, let's calm down and have a drink. We haven't seen each other in a long time and…"

"Gary, this doesn't have anything to do with

you. Brian O'Keefe has been a thorn in my cousin's side for years. And now he's trying to ruin what should be a beautiful tribute to her where…"

"What do you know about it, *Robert?*" Brian hissed. "You didn't just want the secret hidden. You wanted it destroyed. Well, I've got it now. Shelly gave it to me. She told me where it is, and you'll never get your hands on it." Brian began to laugh through his tears.

"Brian, come on. Let's take a walk," Gary insisted and put his hand out like a gentleman for Brian to accept.

But the intoxicated man took a step back and waved Gary off. "You always were a do-gooder, Brookes. I guess someone had to be," Brian said as his eyes flooded with more tears.

Gary shook his head and looked Brian in the eye, trying to keep him distracted long enough to get hold of him. Maggie knew Gary would handle it just right if only he could take Brian by the arm. He'd talk to him as if he was soothing a nervous dog on the way to the vet. Brian would listen and relax and probably break down within minutes as Gary led him somewhere else. Outside. Maybe to the police station. But he'd defuse the situation. Maggie was sure of that.

"Yeah, go with the officer before you get yourself hurt," Robert snapped.

Maggie looked at him with shock. She didn't understand how he could be talking this way in front of everyone. Brian was drunk. He had an excuse for his bad behavior, even if it was a pitiful one. A man his age should have known better. But the weight of the murder and the reunion had obviously taken a toll on Brian, and he wasn't thinking clearly. Robert, however, was sober.

At first, Maggie was sure that Brian had let the frustration he was feeling leave him. His shoulders slumped. His head drooped. It looked as if he'd taken a deep breath and let it out slowly. But within the blink of an eye, he charged at Robert, slipping away before Gary could get his hand around Brian's arm. Before anyone could stop it, Brian had tackled Robert, who seemed to have been expecting it.

Fists were flying. All the fellows at the reunion jumped into action to pull the men apart. Gary was shouting that they were both going to be dragged to the station in cuffs. Maggie stepped back to stay clear of the mob. Her mouth had gone dry, but she was sure that if she'd taken a sip of her sweet, sugary drink, she would have thrown up.

This was too much. Two men screaming and

swearing at one another in the middle of what was supposed to be a party. Maggie wanted nothing to do with this. She felt her way along the wall and inched closer and closer to the back gym exit.

Gary was her dearest friend, and she wanted to help. But what could she do? Jump into the center of this brawl? That was no place for her. Some of the other women she'd gone to school with tried to pull the men apart, shouting their names and screaming for them all to stop. The music had come to a halt. The bartender and the other hired staff were watching with amusement.

"What the heck is going on?"

Maggie jumped and turned to her right to see Joshua standing there. Then she remembered him saying he was going to be at the reunion to work on the lights.

"A fight," Maggie murmured.

"I can see that. What about? Is that Gary? Oh my gosh!" Joshua wasted no time and jumped into the middle of the mess to help Gary, who was trying desperately to get between Brian and Robert. Had it been anyone else, Maggie would have been amused. But now even Joshua had been dragged into this gross display. She couldn't stand it.

"Maggie! Where are you going?" Debbie Morse shouted.

"Maggie, wait!" Christine Whojik called.

Maggie looked at them then at the double doors at the end of the gym. They were just a few paces away, but Maggie felt as if she was making a mad dash for the walls of a prison to escape. With her arms wrapped around her torso, she hurried to the doors, gave them a big push, and left. Her heart was racing. The cold air outside felt good on her skin. The quiet of the neighborhood was a comfort compared to the noise from inside the high school gym.

But Maggie felt awful. She had been drawn into that mess and couldn't understand why. What the heck had Shelly Pinkowski wanted to talk to her about? If she had been asked to tell the truth at this precise moment, Maggie would have said that she'd disliked Shelly. A lot. Perhaps with the intensity of a thousand white-hot suns. If she'd gone the rest of her life without hearing her name, Maggie would have been okay with that. But now she had a drunken Brian O'Keefe channeling Shelly from beyond the grave, singling her out by name like Shelly had done in high school. What mean, conde-scending thing did he have to say to her now?

She wasn't mean or condescending when you saw her at the thrift store, Maggie's conscience replied like a nagging child as she hustled to her car.

This night had started out so nice. Now she was sneaking away like a married woman from a no-tell motel. It made her sick to her stomach.

What was she going to tell Joshua at work tomorrow? Robert hadn't gotten so much as a casual wave goodbye. Maggie felt hungover. All she wanted was her bed, a cup of tea, a new book to read, and some quiet. But she couldn't even get that because she was still holed up at the B&B.

Chapter 16

I t was sunny and clear when the sun peeked through the curtains of Maggie's room. Even in the chilly February weather, the sound of a couple of squawking blue jays could be heard. Maggie sat up in bed. As the memory of the previous night emerged from the fog of sleep, she squinted as if it was too bright to focus on. What an ordeal.

You didn't do anything wrong, her conscience whispered. *You've got nothing to feel embarrassed about.*

As she swung her feet over the side of the bed and stood, the comforting creak of the hardwood floor beneath the area rug brought her into the present moment. Maggie had new clothes to wear from Mrs. Peacock and decided that with her new outfit, she was going to have a new attitude for this new day. Her conscience was right. She didn't have anything to feel embarrassed about. She wasn't the one who'd had too much to drink, nor had she charged anyone or started throwing punches.

No. Brian O'Keefe just singled you out of everyone else at the reunion and announced that Shelly had had something for you. Or wanted to say something to you. That's all. You were just named out loud. In front of everyone. By a friend of a murder victim.

As she peered outside to the beautiful view of the park and the running path, she saw women with strollers, joggers, a couple of bike riders, and one skater. The snow and ice were dripping from the tree branches.

"It must be warm out this morning," she muttered before pursing her lips.

Within no time, she was dressed in a smart pair of casual slacks with a lovely purple V-neck sweater that she hated to cover with her bulky winter coat and scarf. But even with the drips of temperatures above freezing, Maggie knew better than to be deceived by the warm look of the scenery. As soon as she stepped out of the B&B, she was immediately tapped on the head by the drips from the dangling icicles. One drop managed to hit its mark on the back of her neck and snake its way down her back, causing a fit of shivers. That was enough to get her to yank up her hood and peep out from beneath the fuzzy trim like a primordial figure stepping out of a cave.

Once at work, Maggie was hit by the smell of cinnamon buns baking. She walked into the café to find Babs with her baby boy, Earl, on her hip while her husband, Roy, carried a platter filled with the pastries to the counter.

"Good morning," Babs said while bouncing and rocking back and forth. Earl tugged at her bleached-blond pigtails with pink bows at the ends.

"Hi," Maggie said. "Those smell good."

"Don't they? Oh, I can feel my hips getting bigger by the second. Roy made these. It's from an old recipe he found in one of his mama's old cookbooks. Handwritten and dated 1972. Can you believe that?"

"You know bigger hips won't bother me, baby," Roy teased before sliding the cinnamon rolls onto a pretty platter. As he walked back into the kitchen, he gave Babs a pat on her backside, making her giggle.

"That Daddy is just too much," Babs said to Earl, who was staring up at his mama with wide eyes and a trickle of drool down his chin. "Here. Have one. They are delicious." Babs put a roll on a red napkin and held it out for Maggie.

She could not say no. Her stomach growled just as she took a bite. Babs hadn't been lying. The whole pastry literally melted in her mouth.

"Wow. I've never tasted anything like it," Maggie said. "Has Joshua tasted these yet? I'll bet he'll want them in the shop all the time."

"Joshua is at the police station," Babs said before tilting her head to the right. "You didn't know?"

Maggie stopped midbite. "No." She wrinkled her nose and squinted at Babs.

"Yeah. I guess things got out of hand at your reunion last night. I thought you were going to that. Did you change your mind?"

"No," Maggie swallowed, suddenly no longer hungry for even the most scrumptious dessert she'd ever tasted.

"You must have missed it. There was a brouhaha."

"A what?" Maggie asked even though she knew what a brouhaha was. She was just shocked and worried and embarrassed and confused all at once. Why was Joshua at the police station? Where was

Robert? For that matter, where was Brian O'Keefe? Why hadn't Gary called her? He knew where she was staying.

"A brawl. I guess one of your classmates, Brian something-or-other, had a little too much liquid courage and started a fight," Babs said just as Roy appeared with another platter of rolls.

"Yeah. I saw that," Maggie said softly. "But I left just as everyone was jumping in to pull Brian and Robert apart."

"Oh. Yeah. Well, that wasn't the end of it. After the kerfuffle was split up, the men all retreated to their separate corners, but the shouting match continued, and threats were made all around. Next thing you know, at the crack of dawn, that Brian guy was found lying in the driveway of that house on Campbell that you like," Babs said. "He's in the hospital. They don't know if he's going to make it."

"What?" Maggie gasped.

"Yup. Someone wasn't through with him at the reunion. He was beaten badly," Babs added. "According to what Roy told me, which he heard from our neighbor, he'd been lying in the driveway since early this morning. On top of his injuries, he had hypothermia because he had no coat and was just lying there. Even if he does live, the doctors might have to amputate a couple fingers."

Maggie's mouth went dry, and her hands were tingling as if they'd suddenly fallen asleep. All she could think was that she needed to talk to Joshua. Better yet, Gary. He'd tell her what was going on. Joshua couldn't have had anything to do with Brian getting a beating. Heck, a dozen guys had jumped into the melee.

Robert was one of them too. In fact, he was singled out by Brian just like you were, Maggie recalled. No. Robert wasn't like that. He'd walked away from Brian during their spat in the hallway at the B&B. He was a gentleman and classy. He would never have stooped to the level of a common barroom brawl. That was not to say he might not have gotten a couple licks in. But Robert wouldn't have done something like this.

Rich Murphy, on the other hand... Maggie had almost completely forgotten about him. He and Brian had exchanged words that night when she was hiding behind the registration desk. Rich had also been drinking last night. Maybe the two of them had had another argument.

Maggie's mind was spinning by the time she opened the bookshop. Nervously, she paced up and down the floor between the bookshelves and around what had been Mr. Whitfield's tiny office. She rang up two customers wrong, tried to shelve the latest crime-seller in the Western section, and nearly tripped over Poe not once but twice because she wasn't watching where she was going.

Finally, after the first two hours of work felt like they took five hours to go by, Maggie saw Joshua walking past the display window. He opened the door for two ladies coming in, smiling and joking with them as if he hadn't a care in the world.

"What took you so long?" Maggie whispered as she rushed up to him.

"Why? What's the matter with you? Did something break? Please don't tell me a pipe broke. I can't deal with another unexpected expense. I mean, we can. We're doing fine. But I'd just like to have a breather, you know what I mean?" he said as he started to unzip his coat.

"Babs said you were at the police station. What?" Maggie shook her head, her hands out, palms up, and shoulders hunched.

"Oh, that. Yeah. I was at the police station. Gary had to question me. That guy at your reunion last night met with an unfortunate accident. They think he might die," Joshua said.

"You don't seem upset about it," Maggie replied.

Joshua cleared his throat. "I didn't do anything to him. I was dropping off the coffee for the reunion party, and so I was there trying to help break things up. All I saw was him drunk, yelling at you, yelling at your friend Robert. Then a fight broke out that *he* instigated. By the time the whole thing was broken up, he was escorted to the door and told not to come back. That's it."

Maggie swallowed hard. "That's all?"

"That's all I know. The person who beat the tar out of him knows a little more. But I couldn't say who that was. From the looks of it, he didn't have too many friends to begin with. So it could be anybody. Just not me." Joshua winked.

Maggie let out a breath she hadn't even known she was holding. What about Robert? He hadn't seen Maggie leave the reunion. She hadn't even said goodbye.

How could you? He was fighting, her conscience snapped.

At least Joshua wasn't in any trouble. Why was she so worried about Joshua anyway?

"Why are you so worried about me?"

Joshua's question made Maggie look around as

if her subconscious had suddenly punched a hole into the real world and was asking her questions everyone could hear.

"What? I'm not worried about you," she snapped right back as if he'd asked her an inappropriate question about her underthings.

"That sounded like worry," Joshua replied.

"Well, it wasn't."

"Are you sure? Because I think you might have been a little worried."

"I wasn't worried. And If I was, it was only because we've got a shipment of books coming today, and I don't know where you want them." Maggie huffed and crossed her arms as she watched Joshua hang up his coat in the little office.

He was the most handsome man she'd ever seen in blue jeans and a button-down flannel. When he reached for the tool belt that he'd left on the desk, she turned away as if he'd just removed his shirt. Her cheeks blazed.

"Yeah, right," Joshua replied and turned to face her.

Maggie put her hands on her hips and shifted from her right foot to her left. "I don't even know why this is an issue for you. It's like you are just looking for a reason to argue with me."

"No. I never want to argue. You always argue with me." Joshua put his hands on his hips.

"That's not true."

"Yes, it is."

"See, you just proved yourself wrong because you are trying to fight with me over who picks fights with whom. You are picking a fight," Maggie said, looking over the frames of her glasses at Joshua.

"I'm not picking a fight. You are because I asked why you were worried about me." Joshua shook his head.

"I wasn't worried about you," Maggie lied.

"You know, Margaret, you are too much. I don't have all day to argue with you."

"See, you just admitted *you* are arguing with *me*." Maggie lifted her chin in triumph.

"You know… I ought to… just get back to work doing something." Joshua ran his hand through his hair and stomped past Maggie into the café.

Maggie smiled to herself. She loved it when Joshua got all flabbergasted. He was so cute when he didn't know what to say.

He's still your boss. Who calls their boss cute? Only weirdos. Come on, Mags, get back on the clock. There's been a murder and now an attack perpetrated on two separate classmates, and your name has been mentioned by both.

Focus, Maggie's conscience said quietly within the confines of her brain.

It was nearly quitting time when Gary finally appeared at the bookstore. Maggie had finished her tasks for the day and was flipping through a book on fish of the Mississippi River that had incredibly detailed hand-drawn pictures of the creatures when he set off the bells on the door. She immediately slammed the book shut.

"Where have you been?" she whispered.

"At the station. I had to interview half of our class who were at the reunion last night. Which brings me to you. Where did you sneak off to?" Gary looked annoyed.

"You saw what was going on there. It was a mess. I didn't want any part of it, so I slipped out the side door," she said, feeling horrible. "It isn't like I could have jumped into the pile of flying fists and gotten anyone to stop."

"Rich Murphy said you met up with him later last night. Is that true?" Gary asked.

He'd placed both hands on the edge of the counter and looked down at the floor as the words came out of his mouth. Then, when he looked up into Maggie's eyes, she could see he was almost afraid to hear the answer. She wasn't sure why.

"What? Of course it's not true. Rich Murphy? I wouldn't take a sip from the same glass as him, let alone do anything else. Why would he say that?" Maggie huffed.

"Obviously, he's lying about something. Where he went last night after the reunion, for starters," Gary replied. "Now, I have to ask you another hard question. Were you with Robert last night? He disappeared right after the fight too."

Maggie shook her head. "Did he say I was?"

"No. It's just that he's been paying a lot of attention to you, and he's not from around here, and..." Gary trailed off. He looked at Maggie with concern in his eyes. "He's got an ax to grind with half our class, and his cousin was murdered, and it's obvious he's sweet on you. It makes for an interesting set of circumstances. That's all."

"I wasn't with him either. I was back at the B&B, tired of all of this and wishing I was in my cottage. I wish every familiar face would go back to where it came from and leave Fair Haven alone." Maggie sighed.

"Even me?" Gary asked.

Maggie smiled and shook her head. "Never you," she replied barely above a whisper. Gary had been her friend for so many years she couldn't imagine Fair Haven without him. Plus, she had to admit that each year he got a little older, he got a little more distinguished and handsome in his uniform.

That reply made him smirk and lean back a little. "I hate to do this to you, Mags, but I've got to ask you about last night. Tell me what you saw, what you heard, and anything that might be helpful," Gary said.

Maggie hopped up onto her stool and told Gary how she had gotten to the reunion, what she did after she arrived, who she spoke to, and all the way until she slipped out unnoticed.

"That's it?" Gary asked.

"That's it."

"You didn't run into anyone on your way back to the B&B? You didn't see anyone there? Nothing out of the ordinary?" Gary asked.

Maggie shook her head. "Have you got anything to go on? If you are asking me questions, the answer might be no." Maggie scratched the side of her nose then squinted.

"Not much. There are a few details that keep needling me," Gary replied.

"Like what?"

"Like why Jude and Joan Galloway were seen

skulking around the Hallas house the other night. Brian O'Keefe gets the living daylights beaten out of him and is found in the driveway. Shelly's death. And now I'm starting to wonder if Mrs. Hallas wasn't also a victim of foul play," Gary said.

"Do you really believe that?"

"I don't know. All I know is I want you to steer clear of that house on Campbell. I know you like it and think it's pretty, but I get the feeling there is something wrong with it," Gary said. He tugged up the zipper of his coat and pulled a stocking cap onto his head.

"You can't be serious. What are you thinking? Like a curse?"

"Doesn't it seem like it? A lot of bad has happened since the owner of that house passed. You know me, Mags. I'm not one to fall for superstitions, but you gotta admit it's all a little strange," Gary replied with a nod. He gave Maggie a wink and left the bookshop.

Maggie locked the door behind him and turned the "*Open. Come on in*" sign to its "*Sorry. We're closed*" side.

Gary hadn't realized what he'd done, but now that the seed had been planted, she had a weed of curiosity growing like crazy in the back of her mind. Was the house on Campbell cursed? Robert had said it was built like the Winchester house with strange rooms and cubbies. Had Mrs. Hallas thought she had to hide from something? Or had she been nothing more than an eccentric old woman?

All these thoughts raced through her head as she made her way back to the B&B. Once there, she thought she'd take a chance and try and sneak into the Hallas house later.

Who do you think you are? Catwoman? You aren't a burglar, nor do you have any tools that would help you pick a lock or slip a window, and even if you did, you wouldn't know how to use them, that little voice in her head scolded. It was true. But as Maggie walked into the B&B, she couldn't help but stop on the second landing, down the hall from where Brian O'Keefe's room had been. She wondered if Gary and the police had already searched the room. The place was quiet. There weren't a lot of people coming and going.

After a couple of deep breaths as if she was getting ready to dive into cold water, Maggie tiptoed down the hallway and up to the door that Brian had been hanging out of the previous night as he exchanged barbs with Robert, and gently knocked.

After a few seconds of no movement or sound, she knocked again. Still nothing.

Of course there isn't any sound. Brian is in the hospital, she reminded herself. With sweaty hands, she took hold of the doorknob and gave it a turn. To her surprise, it opened with a loud click that made her wince. She looked to both ends of the hallway to make sure no one was going to come running. The coast was clear. Carefully, she opened the door and slipped inside, shutting herself in darkness before sliding her hand along the wall for the light switch. When she snapped it on, she gasped.

Chapter 17

Back in high school, Brian O'Keefe had not been someone Maggie had had any interest in being around. He'd never done anything to her personally. He was what she and Sandy would have called a perfect follower. Always wearing the right clothes, expensive shoes, and a devilish glint in his eyes, he seemed to fit in with the popular cliques. Plus, his last name did not help disprove the stereotype of Irishmen being big drinkers. He had been the first through the front door and the last to leave any parentless party that had taken place during their high school years. At least, that had been the rumor. As far as she could see, Maggie didn't think much had changed.

Still, like Shelly with her horribly condescending

attitude, Maggie didn't think Brian O'Keefe should have been hurt for his faults. Something was obviously wrong with him. A pain in his mind and heart that he wasn't coping very well with had driven him to this state.

But what Maggie was looking at in his room was either the sign of a really depressed mentality, or someone had already been there, searching madly for something. Clothes were strewn all around the floor and across the unmade bed. The mattress was shifted, exposing the box spring underneath. Drawers were wide open. Two suitcases and a duffle bag gaped, their contents dumped out. It looked as if a tornado had hit the room.

"What could someone have been looking for? Or did Brian do all this? I don't know," Maggie whispered as she carefully stepped over a pair of sweatpants and a set of gym shoes.

She looked inside the luggage and saw that it was completely empty, just like the duffle bag. The door to the bathroom was open a slim crack. She peeked inside and saw nothing had been disturbed in there. Either Brian had an affection for water closets and kept his neat, or the person who had ransacked the rest of the suite hadn't bothered with it.

"Why? They weren't looking for his razors and shave cream, I guess," Maggie muttered as she pushed the bathroom door open and stepped inside the small room.

There was a shower with a curved shower rod dangling a white plastic shower curtain, a small podium sink with scalloped edges, and a mirror in a leafy gold frame above that. Nothing out of the ordinary jumped out at her. Just a couple of towels on the floor.

Maggie was about to leave when something made her peek behind the door. A simple black backpack hung from a hook, with a towel next to it. When she lifted the backpack, it had some weight to it. Quickly, Maggie pulled the zipper back and looked inside. There was an unopened bottle of water, a copy of their senior yearbook, some gum, miniature bottles of mouthwash, peppermint Altoids, and a toothbrush and tube of toothpaste. Down at the bottom was a small spiral notebook. Maggie grabbed it before hanging the backpack on the hook again. It clanged against the door. Maggie took one more look inside the bag and found a small travel bottle of whiskey.

"That explains the gum, toothbrush, mouthwash, and Altoids." Maggie nodded.

He'd been drinking a lot over the past couple of days. When she looked at his notebook, she felt a twinge of guilt. From the doodles on the outside, she could tell that this had become a constant companion of his, a place where he turned to be completely honest and vulnerable. His journal of feelings and fears and maybe even hopes. When she flipped open to the first page, there was a crude doodle of a woman with abnormally large breasts. Maggie rolled her eyes and let out a sigh.

"Some men are nothing more than tall eight-year-old boys," she said before wrinkling her nose and flipping to the next page. There were other scribbles of shapes, hatching, and a never-ending string of loop-de-loops. In between these drawings were Brian's thoughts in unfinished paragraphs, familiar lines from songs, and what looked like original poetry. As Maggie read the words, she cringed. Brian was not a poet. But it was obvious he was trying to convey his feelings as best he could.

These meant something to him. I shouldn't judge how good they are but rather how honest they are. Maggie had no doubt that Brian was really struggling with his addiction.

She continued to look through the book and found several pages with lists of things on them.

Lists of movies, songs, places, and names. That was where she first saw her name.

"Margaret Bell? Why am *I* in here? Why is my name written in Brian O'Keefe's AA journal? This is weird," she grumbled to herself.

She wasn't sure if she felt scared or mad at the fact that her name had now popped up in not one but two lists composed by people she had gone to high school with. What had they been up to?

Just as she was about to sit down on the toilet seat cover and continue reading, Maggie heard foot-steps and a voice outside the door.

"Yeah. I told you already, she didn't talk to me. I don't think it's necessary."

"Look. I don't care what you think. Just find it."

"Fine. I'll call you when I have it."

Maggie couldn't place the second voice. But she most certainly recognized the first voice as that of Rich Murphy. What was he doing here? Who he with? And what would he say when he found Maggie there? Thinking quickly, she stepped back into the bathroom and slipped behind the shower curtain before crouching in the tub, her knees to her chest and her arms wrapped tightly around the journal. She held her breath.

"Now, where is this thing?" Rich muttered. "I

don't even know why I'm looking for it. It doesn't have anything to do with me," he hissed to himself.

As far as Maggie could tell, there wasn't anyone else in the room with him. Whomever he'd been talking to in the hallway must have continued on his way.

Rich closed the door behind him, and Maggie could hear him tearing through all the clothes scattered around on the floor and the bags that she had already looked into. She hadn't seen anything out of the ordinary. But whatever Rich was looking for, it was making him madder by the minute when he kept coming up empty-handed. Finally, he pushed the bathroom door open and stepped onto the tiled floor.

At that precise moment, Maggie's thighs decided to start tingling. Then they started to ache, as did her back from being hunched over. Her lips stayed dry no matter how many times she licked them. But she didn't dare move. With wide eyes, she waited, expecting him to throw aside the shower curtain, point at her, and shout "Aha!" But instead, he just continued to mumble to himself.

"How am I supposed to know what he did with it? He never went anywhere without it. Stupid notebook," Rich hissed.

Maggie looked down at the journal she was holding and clutched it tighter. What could be in it that was so important? Pushing through the pain in her strained legs, Maggie managed to stay completely still as Rich continued to shuffle around the small room. Her legs felt like they were going numb. If she jumped up, she couldn't be sure she'd stay on her feet. Better to just stay put.

"Come on, man!" Rich shouted before yanking the door.

Maggie listened intently and heard him lift the backpack from the hook. Rich was looking for the journal she was holding. She was sure of it. Sweat coated her forehead and made her hands clammy. Even though she was sure that if he listened hard enough, Rich could hear her heart pounding, Maggie remained stone still.

"Well, it's not a total waste," he said. The sound of a twist cap, a gulp, and a long *Ahhhhh* let Maggie know that Rich had drunk the small bottle of whiskey. Then came a thud as he tossed the bottle into the wastebasket.

Just as she was sure he was going to leave the bathroom, Maggie was engulfed in silence. He was still there. He hadn't moved. Was he staring at the shower curtain? Did he hear her breathing? Had he known she was there all along? Maggie waited as her imagination ran wild with crazy scenarios in which Rich was going to drag her out of the shower and do to her what he had done to Shelly. He was just toying with her now. He knew she was there. He was waiting for her to cough or sneeze. Her legs were burning from being so awkwardly bent for what felt like hours.

Just then, her stomach rumbled. She hadn't eaten anything lately.

For sure, he heard that. He'd have to be deaf not to, Maggie thought as she bit her lip, waiting to have her hiding place exposed.

But nothing happened. The waiting was torture. Again, Maggie wondered what was the worst that could happen if she just stood up, flung the curtain aside, and ran out. The pain in her legs was making her desperate. She wasn't thinking clearly as the desire to relieve the pain became too much to ignore.

But Rich is a killer. You know he is the one who killed Shelly. Probably the one who put Brian in the hospital. If you move now, he will have no problem doing the same to you, her conscience scolded.

Finally, there was a knock on the door, and Rich

snapped out of whatever trance he had been in to quietly answer it.

"I'm telling you, it isn't here" was all Maggie heard before the door shut again. She listened hard, but the voices on the other side of the door were muffled. They weren't in Brian's room anymore.

After a series of clicks in her knees, Maggie slowly stood up. Every muscle in her legs and back screamed with relief, and she let out a deep breath.

She looked down at the journal then slowly peeled back the shower curtain and climbed out of the tub. Still listening, she stuck her head out of the bathroom. The voices were just outside the door. Maggie looked all around. If they decided to come back in, Maggie would have nowhere to hide from two people on a search-and-possibly-destroy mission. She looked at the curtains hanging in front of the French doors. Like the window in her room, it had a small balcony on the other side.

This isn't an episode of I Love Lucy. *This is real life, Margaret. You can't climb out there*, she thought. But the voices weren't leaving, and Maggie was sure that any second, the doorknob was going to jiggle before it opened, and Rich Murphy and whomever he was with would storm in and discover her. It was a real possibility that she would end up like Brian O'Keefe if not worse.

Maggie bit her bottom lip, tiptoed to the window, and carefully flipped the latch open. The cold air rushed into the room through the tiny crack. It smelled like rain might be coming.

Of course it might rain. As soon as you step out onto that balcony, it's going to start. You know it. That's your luck, her conscience shouted.

Maggie heard Rich speaking. "I'm telling you, I looked. There wasn't anything in there. He probably left it at Shelly's. Or maybe…" He sounded frustrated. Whomever he was talking to was much calmer. The reply was muffled.

Maggie opened the window and stepped outside. The balcony was only eighteen inches wide. The trellis next to it was covered with dried vines and ice. The view of the park wasn't as good as the one from her window, but Maggie had to admit this was a lovely panorama. That was what she was trying to focus on instead of the fact that she was standing on a balcony not designed for a person to stand on. Her weight made the decking sag beneath her, which made her heart skip. Reaching behind her, she pulled the curtains back into place and was about to shut the window when Rich Murphy came back into the room.

"Go ahead! Look around! What do you think I'm going to do? Keep that notebook for myself? Nothing but a bunch of crazy on the pages," Rich barked.

"Shut up!" hissed the other man in the room.

Maggie squinted and eased herself to the farthest corner of the balcony, pushing her back against the brick of the building. As long as no one stuck their head out the window, no one would know she was there.

There was a rumbling sound in the room like furniture was being moved around. Footsteps tromped back and forth. Maggie was starting to shiver. She hoped no one would notice her, think she was a jumper, and call the police.

This isn't so bad, she mused as she peeked in the direction of the window. A couple of doves landed on the balcony railing. Their wide, round yellow eyes judged her. What was she doing there? Even they seemed to know that people weren't supposed to be on this ledge.

Just as that thought entered her mind, the balcony suddenly dipped. Maggie pressed her back harder against the brick while pulling her heels to the wall, hoping to relieve some of the stress of her weight.

Just then, she heard the curtains slide open. The sound of the window being shut completely and the tiny latch slipping into place echoed like a crack of thunder.

Don't panic. You can jump if you must. Her mind began to run like a hamster in a wheel. She peered carefully over the edge of the balcony. The ground appeared to swirl up around her, making her woozy. She gulped the air and slapped her back against the brick, standing motionless as the rain started to fall.

Okay, too far to jump. But I can climb. Her heart thudded with relief as she looked to the trellis. It was sturdy and could certainly hold a young woman her size, couldn't it? Between it and the thick vines that had wound their way throughout the lattice spaces, it was probably a lot sturdier than she needed.

Maggie listened at the window. She could hear quiet talking but didn't think the speakers would notice her if she hunched over to hobble two steps to the other side of the balcony. Once there, she braced her back against the brick again and wrinkled her nose as she peered over the edge. It wasn't that high. Just two stories. It wasn't as if she was balancing on the five-inch concrete ledge of a skyscraper with pigeons and high gusts of wind to contend with. This was just a little trellis she'd have to climb down like a ladder. Better than a ladder, really, because there were more places for her to put her hands and feet.

The temperature was dropping. It was now or never. As she scanned the corner of the park, she could see a jogger just about to pass by. She didn't want anyone to see her imitation of Spider-Man creeping down the building. When she finally thought the coast was as clear as it was ever going to be, Maggie stuffed Brian O'Keefe's notebook down her shirt, zipped her coat, and pulled up her hood. She quickly swung her right leg over the side and hooked it in the lattice, feeling for footing with her penny loafer. She did the same with her left and felt a rush of adrenaline through her veins. She was actually scaling the B&B. It was like something out of a movie.

As the ground got closer and closer, Maggie felt braver and braver. It was no big deal if anyone had seen her. She had her reasons for climbing out the window and down this brick wall. No one needed to know them—that was for sure. Her confidence overflowed. When she got roughly three feet from the ground, she jumped and made what she imagined was an Olympic gold-medal dismount that no trained gymnast could have done any better.

Brushing off her slacks and the front of her jacket, Maggie lifted her chin and walked around the B&B to the front sidewalk. No one had seen her act of bravery. No one would believe her if she told them, and how would she explain that she'd snuck into Brian O'Keefe's room and absconded with his journal? She couldn't. So no one would ever know of her astounding feat but her. It was a delicious secret to keep.

Chapter 18

After strolling through the front door as if she hadn't just succeeded in a feat of derring-do, Maggie waved to Mrs. Burnside, who wore a lovely maroon blouse with pearls around her wrists and throat.

"Happy Valentine's Day," Mrs. Burnside said in her throaty contralto.

"Yes. Yes," Maggie stuttered. "I'd forgotten all about it. Happy Valentine's Day to you too. Have you seen the display at the bookstore?"

"Of course I have. Everyone is talking about it and how unfair it is that Joshua Whitfield has the most talented window dresser in Fair Haven."

Mrs. Burnside was so glamorous that Maggie could have stared at her for hours as she flitted about behind the desk as if her feet barely touched the ground. But as it was, she wanted to read what was in Brian's journal, which was scraping against her stomach at this very moment.

"What can I do?" Maggie blushed. "Have a nice night, Mrs. Burnside."

"Wait. You had a delivery." Mrs. Burnside stepped into the walk-in closet that was separated from the front desk by an elegant lace curtain. She reappeared with a bouquet of red roses in a beveled glass vase.

Maggie's eyes popped as her jaw dropped. "Who are they from?" Maggie asked.

"I'm sorry, dear, I didn't read the card," Mrs. Burnside replied with a hint of scandal in her voice and her right eyebrow arched high.

Maggie knew her smile was crooked, putting her embarrassment on full display as she reached for the vase. It was heavy. The smell of the roses was intoxicating. As she made her way out of the lobby and up the stairs to her small room, she couldn't help feeling special. Once in her room, she set the flowers on the nightstand and withdrew the card.

Pick you up at 8 p.m.
For a Valentine we won't ever forget.

—Robert

Maggie smiled and leaned over to smell the sweet fragrance again. Then she looked at the clock. It was five thirty. She sat down on the bed and fished Brian's notebook out from under her shirt. As much as she would have liked to daydream about Robert and spend the next two and a half hours planning what to wear, she couldn't. Curiosity about what Brian had written was overwhelming. She skimmed the first few pages before even taking her coat off and began to read.

At first, Brian's journal was a lot of lists. Painful memories. Sad experiences. Loss of friends and family. The more she read, the more Maggie felt guilty about having stolen the notebook. But then the entries became more eloquent. At least, as eloquent as Brian O'Keefe could be.

AUGUST 8—I didn't like who I was. I was a rude jerk. But I still wanted a drink even though I knew what it would do. What's wrong with me?

AUGUST 24—I tried to say I was sorry to Fran. She slammed the door in my face. I can't blame her.

. . .

September 16—You won't believe who I saw at the meeting. Shelly. After all this time, Shelly was there. It was good to see her. It was embarrassing at first but then we laughed. It was the first time in weeks maybe longer that I laughed at anything.

MAGGIE CONTINUED TO READ. It was like watching *Rocky*. Brian O'Keefe was a nobody. A nothing. Then, he decided to take a chance. Maggie realized she was rooting for him. On the pages, he wrote in his limited vocabulary how he wanted to do better. So did Shelly. All of the information she was drinking in made Maggie feel a little guilty about her negative thoughts toward Shelly Pinkowski and Brian O'Keefe. But then she came across her name. It was part of a list.

"Step nine of the twelve-step program. I get it," Maggie whispered. Shelly and Brian had made lists of people to apologize to. Although Maggie wasn't on any list of Brian's, he had written that Shelly had included her. It had been about high school and had nothing to do with her drinking. But according to Brian's notes, she wanted to fix everything.

. . .

JANUARY 2—THERE was no changing her mind. That was one thing about Shelly. When she made a decision, it was useless to try to talk her out of it. Maggie Bell probably doesn't even remember who Shelly is or what she's talking about. But it's what Shelly wants to do. Who am I to stop her?

MAGGIE CLOSED the notebook and let out a long sigh. Even though she didn't think it made any sense, she was touched that Shelly had thought to make things right with her. Why she hadn't done it at the thrift store when they ran into each other, Maggie didn't know. Maybe she had more to say than "Sorry for being rude to you in high school."

Why did there seem to be so much hoopla from Gary about Maggie's name being on some kind of list they'd found with Shelly at the time of her death? Why did Rich Murphy want this notebook so badly? Maggie flipped through the rest of the pages. She saw the names of Jude and Joan Galloway. The address of the Hallas house on Campbell Street. A sketch of the building with arrows and circles and stars scribbled all over it, like a treasure map of sorts.

"What did Brian care about the house or the Galloways?" Maggie muttered.

Nothing more was written in the journal about it. There was only one way to find out. She'd have to go see him at the hospital. She looked at the clock on the dresser. She'd have about two hours to get there, ask him about the notebook, and get back here to meet Robert. There was also the fact that he'd been beaten badly. There was no guarantee that he'd even be able to speak, let alone answer any questions.

The hospital wasn't that far away. If she drove just a hair over the speed limit, she should get there in no time. She couldn't be sure of visiting hours, but she was willing to take a chance. There would be no rest until she found out why he was interested in the Galloways and the Hallas house.

Maybe it's as simple as he wanted to move there, Maggie thought as she got into her car. *Maybe he wanted to move back home to get away from the life he had in California.* It was possible. Maggie dreamed up a million other possibilities as she drove.

There was a soft rain falling that made the road slick. The temperature was warm for February. The reflections of the streetlights glistened off the pavement. After a few left turns and a stretch of road with a pharmacy, a gas station, and a payday loan office, Maggie saw the words EMERGENCY ENTRANCE in bright red letters.

"This isn't really an emergency," Maggie muttered. She drove around and found a parking spot near an entrance she hoped would be close to wherever they'd put Brian.

"He's in intensive care. Are you a family member?" the woman behind the information desk asked sternly. Her nametag read Mrs. Black.

"Uh, er, not exactly," Maggie muttered. "We… are engaged… or, well…" Quickly, Maggie hid her ringless left hand just as Mrs. Black's eyes darted to it. "Actually, we're engaged to be engaged. If that makes any sense."

Mrs. Black's face didn't move as she looked down at her desk behind a high counter. Maggie was sure she was going to say that she knew Maggie was lying and that she had better beat it out of the hospital before she called security. Instead, she handed her a purple piece of paper.

"This is your pass. You must return it on your way out. Visiting hours end in twenty minutes.

Elevators are around the corner," Mrs. Black ordered.

That was easy, Maggie thought. The purple piece of paper listed Brian's name, floor, and room number.

Maggie hurried to the elevator before Mrs. Black could change her mind. Maggie's back was unnaturally straight, her chin was pulled into her neck, and her eyes darted from side to side as she shuffled to the first available elevator. Once inside with two other hospital visitors, she pressed the number four on the panel and slipped into the back corner.

Only once she stepped off the elevator did she let her breath out. Brian was in room IC-422. Maggie continued her Frankenstein-like walk down the corridors until she came to the number she was looking for. The door was slightly open. She stood there for a moment, wondering why she was doing this. He probably couldn't talk. He might have been so heavily sedated that he wouldn't be able to talk even if he wanted to.

Finally, Maggie took a deep breath, let it out, and gently knocked on the door. There was no answer.

"Hello?" she called softly as she pushed the door

open. When she stepped in, she saw a monitor with wires drooping from it to the bed in which a person lay. Maggie took a few steps in then stopped in her tracks. A gasp tried to escape her lips, but she choked it back.

Brian was nothing more than a black-and-blue mess. There was a bandage around his head. His right eye was swollen shut. His bottom lip was puffy. One arm was in a cast. His chest was wrapped but not encased in plaster.

"Shelly?" he muttered and blinked his one good eye open.

"Hi, Brian. No. It's Maggie. Maggie Bell. Gary Brookes told me you were here. Uh... what the heck happened?" Maggie asked.

"Shelly. We shouldn't have come. This was a dumb idea," Brian slurred.

"No. I'm Maggie. Remember me? We were both at the reunion last night. Do you remember going?" Maggie hadn't expected Brian to be conscious. Now that he was and was confused about whom he was talking to, she was frozen.

"We never should have come. The twelve steps didn't say anything about getting ourselves killed," Brian muttered. "I was afraid this was going to happen."

"What, Brian? You were afraid that what was going to happen?"

He swallowed hard and sank into his pillow. His face and exposed skin were the only things with any color across the whole bed. The stark whiteness of the bedding put a spotlight on his injuries. Maggie shivered. Who could do this to another person?

Without thinking, she walked to the rolling table at the side of the bed, upon which sat a pitcher and a plastic cup. She poured him some water, plunked a straw into it, and held it to his lips. Brian took a sip, licked his lips, and let out a sigh. It helped him focus. He blinked and finally focused on Maggie.

"Maggie. You need to go," he said softly.

"No. You told me last night at the reunion that you were going to speak for Shelly. What did you mean by that?" she asked softly, as if she was trying to coax a kitten out from underneath a chair.

"I looked for you. You left. Why did you leave?" Brian asked with his head raised just a little off the pillow.

"Because... a... fight broke out," Maggie replied. Didn't he remember?

"No one would have hurt you. No one was after *you*. Not yet, anyway." He stated it as if Maggie should have been ready to step out of her heels, pull off her earrings, and join the rumble. The whole idea confused her. Brian rolled his eyes and let out another sigh.

"You said you were going to speak *for* her. Did Shelly have something to say to me? You mentioned you were sorry? What about?" Maggie continued.

After all, she hadn't started the fight. He had. She had just been there to make a quick appearance and go. He had drawn her into the melee by singling her out. As she mulled over her actions from the night before, feeling guilty for being a coward and leaving, Brian appeared to get a healthy dose of sedative.

His eyes glazed, and he blinked slowly. "What? Maggie? No. Shelly never told Maggie what she wanted to say." Brian sounded like he was still drunk.

It was the medicine he was on, Maggie knew. But just as if he'd had too much to drink, she wasn't going to get anywhere. Not tonight.

"Do you remember what she wanted to say?"

Brian's eyes started to close, and his muscles relaxed as he sank deeper into the bed.

"Maybe I'll come see you tomorrow." Maggie turned to leave.

In an instant, Brian reached out, clutched her

hand, and held her tightly. "Shelly told you about the secret panel, right? She told you that the documents were in there and to mail them to the attached address, right?" Brian opened wide his good eye.

"No. I don't know what you are talking about," Maggie replied as she tried to pull her hand away. For a guy who was in critical condition, he was still very strong.

"Get those documents before he does. Mail them. It's history. It's the truth, no matter how ugly. Shelly had accepted it. Why couldn't he?" Brian said with his lips drawn down at the corners in was a sad, bewildered frown.

"Okay," Maggie agreed, but only to get Brian to let her hand go.

"He thinks Joan Galloway knows. She doesn't. She's a good person. Don't let him do to her what he's done to Shelly. Don't... let... him..." Brian slipped under the influence of the medications that dripped slowly from two IV bags hanging from a rolling metal coatrack kind of gadget. This time, it didn't take any strength for Maggie to gently pull her hand away.

She stood there for a couple of seconds, trying to make sense of what he had just said. It was a lot to absorb. Secret panel? Joan Galloway? History? Maggie smoothed the white blanket covering Brian O'Keefe before leaving the room.

As soon as she stepped into the hallway, she saw Rich Murphy and a hospital security guard step off the elevator. She was sure they were headed to Brian's room. Quickly, she turned her back, pulled up her hood, and started walking in the other direction.

"Excuse me." Maggie heard a female voice but paid no attention. Just as she came to a corridor on her left, she looked over her shoulder and saw Rich enter Brian's room. The security guard stayed in the hallway. What was that all about?

"Excuse me, ma'am?" Still, Maggie kept walking, looking over her shoulder while not paying any attention to where she was headed, until she felt a tug on her arm.

"What?" Maggie snapped, pinching her eyebrows down and wrinkling her nose.

"You can't go down here, ma'am. This area is restricted," a nurse in snug lavender scrubs and gardening clogs replied with her own eyebrows furrowed.

"Oh. Uh… sorry. Which way are the elevators?"

"That way." The woman pointed in the direction Maggie had just come from. "There's a big sign with an arrow."

"Oh. Yes. I see it now," Maggie replied with a nod before tugging at her hood and heading off in the right direction. As she hurried past the security guard outside Brian's door, she listened. There was nothing. No sound. No talking. Nothing. Not to mention the guard looked as if he had a million better things to do than stand there protecting… who? Brian? Rich? Maggie didn't know and wasn't going to ask. She hustled to the elevators, punched the button, and prayed the doors would slide open before Rich realized Brian wasn't talking.

Once the bell pinged, Maggie stepped inside, pressed the button for the lobby, and pushed herself to the back corner of the elevator compartment. When the doors finally slid shut, she let out a sigh of relief. There was just enough time to meet Robert at the B&B.

Chapter 19

Love was definitely in the air as Maggie parked her car on the street and walked to the B&B entrance. Even though the temperature was crisp and chilly, couples strolled hand in hand, whispering sweetly, smiling, and giggling their way down the sidewalk.

It wasn't that she didn't like Valentine's Day or that she'd been one of those bitter young women who made fun of it because she usually didn't have anyone to spend it with. No. Maggie had never paid much attention to the rosy-colored holiday, because she thought romance should be more than just one special day a year. The library of truly romantic books she had read over the course of her life might have bloated her idea of what love was, but she knew that it wasn't something that she wanted to be over in twenty-four hours. It should pop up like a spring shower or the sweet chirp of a cardinal occasionally to remind people that love was always an option.

What scared Maggie most wasn't putting her heart out there, although she would admit she wasn't keen on wearing it on her sleeve. In fact, if she were to be honest with herself, her heart had been safely wrapped in tissue paper and stuffed in a box in the back of her closet for most of her life. But having felt that kind of love and seeing it wane, become mundane, was her fear.

She didn't know if "love" was the right word to use regarding Robert Hallas. All she knew was that the minute he walked through the door, she couldn't help but smile. He looked so dapper in his long tan coat and earmuffs. His round spectacles gave him such an innocent appearance.

"Are you ready to go?" he asked, offering her his elbow.

She linked her arm through it. "I am." She smiled.

Before she realized it, they were in Robert's car, driving down residential streets. The homes were lovely. Maggie knew most of them and was about to point out Mrs. Donovan's house and Mrs. Peacock's in order to discuss their rivalry and point out her own small cottage. But something told her this wasn't the right time.

"Where are we going?" Maggie asked.

"I've got a surprise in store for you," Robert said and raised his chin slightly.

"Really?" Before Maggie could ask for a hint, they were turning down Campbell Street.

She instantly knew where they were heading, and for some reason, the idea didn't sit well with her. Sure, she would have loved to see the Hallas home and all the décor on the inside. But it was Valentine's Day. She hated to admit she had been expecting dinner somewhere with a menu especially made for two, soft music, and low lighting. Somewhere they could hold hands across the table while they talked.

Don't be silly. Maybe he has that in mind and you will just be doing it in his family home. Her conscience tried to spin the situation.

Yeah, how romantic to take you to a place where one person died of old age, one was murdered, and another was beaten within an inch of his life, her brain interrupted.

Suddenly, she was not all that interested in celebrating Valentine's Day. When they pulled up in front of the Hallas house, Maggie let out a sigh.

"I know. You were expecting dinner at a restaurant," Robert said. He parked the car, turned off the lights and the ignition, and faced her.

"I was," Maggie said.

"There is just a little business we need to address first." Robert cleared his throat. "You know what it is, right?"

Maggie shook her head.

"Come on. Maybe once we are inside where it's warm, you'll remember," Robert said. "Did I tell you how pretty you look tonight?"

"Thanks," Maggie muttered.

Robert hopped out of the driver's seat and hurried to her side, yanking the door open and offering her his hand. She reluctantly took it and didn't like how hard he squeezed her fingers.

Robert pulled her more than escorted her to the front door. He took hold of the knob and turned it, and the door opened easily. Maggie thought it looked as if the lock had been forced. But it was dark and there were shadows, so she couldn't be sure. She didn't want to be sure. If that was the case and Robert had done it, she was in a lot of trouble right now.

The foyer was beautiful, with a lovely design of a fleur-de-lis on the floor. There were paintings of what looked like wild horses on a vast prairie on one side and a Chinese tapestry on the other. There was also an old-fashioned macramé plant holder dangling from the ceiling and a hooked rug in a butterfly pattern underneath a small shelf. It was a mishmash of tasteful and tacky décor that puzzled Maggie.

"Your mom had interesting taste," she said softly. "I always wondered what the inside of this house looked like."

"My mom was crazy," Robert replied.

"Oh, sure. We all think of our parents as a little weird." Maggie chuckled.

"No. I mean she really was. She'd been in and out of the booby hatch a dozen times at least. She said she heard voices and was convinced someone was out to get her."

Robert led Maggie farther into the house. Up ahead, the dining room light was on. Dimmed to give the room a romantic glow, it seemed more ominous to Maggie, as if Robert was trying to make the scene scary.

"What do you mean?"

"Come on, Maggie. You were the one Shelly

kept talking about. She and you shared some information. I know you did. Your name was the only one listed in her wallet. Brian O'Keefe had your name too. But he wouldn't talk either," Robert hissed.

"Robert, I don't know what you are getting at. I saw Shelly at the thrift store, and she mentioned donating her aunt's things. She said she'd see me at the reunion. Then she was killed. And I…"

Suddenly, Maggie remembered her conversation with Shelly in vivid detail. Shelly had mentioned how she was the only one who had cared about her aunt. Her cousins hadn't. Her own children, meaning Robert, hadn't cared what happened to Mrs. Hallas. But here Robert was, acting as if he owned the house and had feelings for it. Something was seriously wrong. Maggie's heart began to race.

"Where are they?" Robert asked as he pulled Maggie toward the dining room. There were candles on the table but no food. No wine or sparkling cider. Just the flickering candles and a rope.

Maggie stared at it as if it might come to life and bite her. "Where are what?" she gasped.

"The records, Maggie. Tell me where the

records are, and we can just go on with our evening like nothing happened," Robert whined.

Maggie said nothing. She searched her memory for any mention of records. She wrinkled her nose and pulled her shoulders up before she began to speak.

"Did you think to check the thrift store? Shelly was dropping off a lot of stuff. Maybe she took in the records you are talking about," Maggie said. "I don't have any records. I don't even have a record player. I wouldn't even know where to buy one nowadays. Do they even make them anymore?"

"Take a seat," he growled.

"I'm okay to stand," Maggie tried.

But Robert yanked her by the hand as he pulled out a dining room chair and nearly flung her into it. "I said take a seat!"

Maggie gripped the armrests. Her back was straight, but her head was down. She was afraid that at any second, Robert was going to get physical. When he knelt in front of her, tenderly taking her hands in his, she held her breath.

"Maggie, don't play dumb. It doesn't suit you. Just tell me where Shelly put the family records, and we can forget everything else. I know my mother had some weird ways. There are secret panels and cubbies all over this place. Some of them have canceled checks in them. Some have old ham sandwiches in them." He chuckled bitterly. "I just haven't been able to find the one with our records in them. I know they are here. I know you know where they are. Tell me."

His voice was softer, almost kind. But when Maggie continued to just stare at him, making no movement and with a blank look on her face, he changed.

"I can't tell you what I don't know," she muttered.

Robert let out a long sigh before standing. With a snap of his arm, he grabbed the rope and wrapped it around Maggie's wrists.

In a book about Harry Houdini, Maggie had learned that he could squirm out of ropes by flexing his muscles as he was tied up. It allowed him just enough literal wiggle room. Maggie did the same, and when Robert was finished, she was shocked to discover that with enough time, she would be able to pull one hand free. She waited and watched her captor shake his head, mumble, and chew his lower lip. He was not the polished, charming Robert she'd known this short time. He was someone else entirely.

Robert casually slid his hands into his pockets and stepped back. Then he walked over to the bar, cans of Schlitz beer on the shelves behind it. Where other people might keep decades-old Scotch or dusty bottles of aged Italian wine, Mrs. Hallas had kept nothing but Schlitz beer.

Maggie wondered if she had drunk any of it or just had it there for aesthetics. It might have been an odd choice, but it suited the décor. There was a breathtaking painting of an old fisherman on the wall next to the bar. Next to it was one of those novelty fish on a plaque that sang when someone got too close to them. All the other decorations were a jumble of styles and time periods. Nothing went together, yet it all seemed to coexist as a colorful patchwork that only Mrs. Hallas could really have appreciated.

"I know what you're thinking," Robert said.

"I doubt that," Maggie replied in a low voice.

Either Robert didn't hear her, or he chose to ignore her. She couldn't be sure which it was.

"You're wondering if you should betray a friend's trust for a man you just met. I'm sorry, Maggie. I shouldn't have barked at you the way I did. This has to be an impossible situation for you. I should have thought of it that way before I came to get you. It's just that time is running short. I don't have a lot of time to court you properly. So I'm asking you to trust me and tell me where the records are. I promise I'll explain everything once I have them."

Robert looked at Maggie with eyes that seemed flat and two-dimensional.

Robert continued to talk about loyalty and friendship and the great personal cost to get the things in life a person wanted. None of it made any sense to Maggie. It was as if a switch had been flipped, and Robert was going to talk and talk until someone or something turned him off again. Then he'd be normal. Then he'd start making sense.

"If your friendship with Shelly meant anything, you'll tell me where those records are hidden. If I mean anything to you, you'll tell me," he finished. He stood there rocking back and forth on his heels.

Maggie swallowed. "I wish I could help. You obviously need it." She cursed herself for her uncontrollable sarcasm. Especially when she saw the grin drop from Robert's face. "But I wasn't friends with Shelly. We didn't like each other in high school. She was a real witch and made it clear I wasn't welcome in her group. No great loss, really."

"What?" Robert winced.

"It's true. She said I had bugs and made fun of me, and all because her boyfriend, Jimmy Bradford, talked to me at a party. Sure, he was cute and all, but I'm no boyfriend stealer." She mumbled that last part more to herself than to Robert and looked down at her hands. The rough rope made her skin itch.

An eerie hush fell over the room. Maggie became acutely aware of the sound of a couple of clocks ticking, the heat hissing through the vents, and a random snap or pop of the house itself settling. She looked up to see Robert staring at her so intently it made Maggie jump in her seat.

"You expect me to believe that?"

"It's the truth. To be honest, I didn't like Shelly at all. Even when I ran into her, I didn't want to exchange words. I could see the same condescending look in her eyes I saw all through high school. But she approached me and began talking about how she was the only one who cared about her aunt. That not even her children cared what happened to her. That was what Shelly said." Maggie blurted the words out then took a deep breath. "Is that true? That you didn't care what happened to your mother?"

Robert shook his head. "You couldn't talk to my

mother." He began to slowly stroll back and forth in front of the bar as if he were giving dictation. "My gosh, between the visits to the head shrinkers and the stints in the asylums, it's a miracle anyone knew she lived here at all."

"What?"

"That's right. My mother had a history of mental illness that could put Norman Bates to shame. She didn't kill anyone as far as I know, but she was talking to walls and doodling with blue crayons between her toes because her arms were in a straitjacket more times than I care to admit. Do you know how it would look if anyone got their hands on those records?"

Maggie felt her stomach fold over on itself. How could someone talk about their mother's mental illness like this? Suddenly, Robert became an ugly, twisted man right before her eyes.

"You don't even care what she was going through," she said.

"Why should I? She didn't care what I was going through! Look at this place! Does this look like the family home of a future congressman? Being coroner is just the start. I've got dreams, Maggie. Do you know what the stain of mental illness in my family could do to my chances of climbing the political ladder?"

Maggie couldn't believe what she was hearing. Then a possibility that was so horrifying, so grotesque she was afraid to utter the words, dawned on her. But as if someone had pulled the lever of a slot machine, everything came tumbling out.

"You killed Shelly, didn't you? She wouldn't give you the records, so you killed her. You thought Brian knew about your family history, and you wanted to put an end to him. Now you've got me and… you've lost your mind."

Robert narrowed his eyes and glared at Maggie. "Don't do this, Maggie. You know as well as I do that the life of a politician's wife is the kind of life girls dream of. You get to play dress-up at all the best parties. You have security to keep people you don't like away. And the respect, my gosh. They'll show you respect you'd never get just selling books at some old bookstore." He smirked. "Maggie, you fit the mold of a perfect politician's wife. You're pretty and smart. But most importantly, you aren't the kind of woman who would draw attention to herself. You'd know your place, and it would be at my side. Not in front of me."

"You didn't deny it." Her voice was just above a whisper.

"Deny what?"

"You killed Shelly."

"When my mother wouldn't hand over the records, I needed to find the only person who would have any knowledge about where they were. Shelly was always sucking up to Mother. Of course, that old biddy told her what secret place she'd hid them in. But Shelly was the same old snob you claimed she was in high school and wouldn't tell me anything," Robert said as he picked at his bottom lip.

It was a disgusting tic that Maggie was finding more and more unnerving. "Did you kill your mother?"

"She was on her last legs anyway. It didn't take much. She was old and frail, and the slightest disruption in her daily routine was enough to send her into shock. That's no way to live," Robert said. "Besides, I wasn't the one who was keeping secrets. It was her. She was hiding things from me. Things she knew I needed. Things that could ruin me. What kind of mother does that?"

"Because murder won't cause anyone to bat an eye. Oh, I see your point." Maggie couldn't stop the words. They were like circus tumblers, jumping, leaping, catapulting out of her mouth.

Her hands were getting sweaty. She knew if she tried, she might be able to pull one hand free. If only Robert would take a walk to another room or even turn his back on her for a few seconds. There was a beautiful marble candleholder with dangling crystals just an arm's length away from her. If she could manage to get free and grab it, she might be able to clunk him on the head and make a break for it. But there was no way she'd be able to outrun him unless she stunned him first.

But the look on Robert's face was enough to quench any flicker of hope she had. He lunged, grabbed her by her bound wrists, and yanked her to her feet.

"We are going to take a walk, starting in the attic and working our way down. If you don't tell me where my mother hid those records by the time we reach the basement, you won't ever be leaving this house," Robert said. His hand clamped on her shoulder, he pushed her out of the dining room and up a flight of stairs.

Maggie had no idea what she was going to do.

Chapter 20

Even with the prospect of her impending doom, Maggie couldn't help but admire all the trinkets and kitsch that filled the attic. There were half a dozen footlockers and hope chests she would have loved to dig through. There were pieces of vintage furniture, thick, tall dressers with unique knobs and handles, gawdy frames around full-length mirrors, and stacks of linens of different colors and patterns. There were boxes marked *Christmas ornaments* and more than one Christmas tree taking up a corner. To rummage through everything would have been a real treat. She kept spotting treasures here and there, but really, all she was doing was pushing the fear from her mind. Those trunks were big enough to hide her body until she mummified. But she couldn't think of that. She didn't dare.

The layer of dust and cobwebs over everything gave it all a romantic yet slightly macabre aura. Still, with Robert becoming more and more unglued, she tried to remain calm by admiring all the pretty things.

"I know there are three or four secret panels up here. Tell me where they are," Robert ordered as he pushed Maggie to the middle of the floor. The boards creaked beneath her feet.

"For the tenth time, Robert, I don't know. You killed the only person who could have helped you," Maggie said.

It probably hadn't been the smartest thing to say. If Robert didn't believe she knew where these secret panels were, he might just end her life right then and there. No one would know where she was. No one had seen her leave the B&B with him. A guy who had sent her flowers for a romantic Valentine's Day wouldn't be a prime suspect. At least, not until he'd had ample time to flee the city or the state. Or even the country.

He's not fleeing the country. He wants to be a congressman. Don't be silly, Mags.

"Where, Maggie?"

"I don't... think she put them up here. I think she put them closer to her bedroom." Maggie hoped the lie sounded believable enough.

When Robert whirled around and stared at her, she was sure he'd seen through her falsehood. But when he smiled, she let out a quiet breath of relief. It was enough to buy her a little more time.

"Now, was that so hard? Just calm down, Maggie. I don't want to hurt you, and I promise this will all be worthwhile in the end. My mother would have liked you. Or she would have thought you were some relative back from the dead to play gin rummy with." Robert laughed at his own cruel comment. "Either way, I'm sure she would have enjoyed your company."

Robert again guided Maggie with his hand on her shoulder to the second floor and his mother's bedroom. It was decorated like a three-year-old girl's birthday cake with ruffles and layers of pink and white satiny fabric along the bed frame, around the base of each lampshade, and across the two windows. The entire bedroom set was in the thick, clunky style of 1960s furniture.

Without giving herself a second to think, she broke away from Robert and dove under the bed.

Even with her wrists bound, she could hold on tight to the wide, immovable legs.

"Maggie, I can wait as long as you can," Robert said as he dropped to one knee and peeked under the ruffles.

"You're sick, Robert! You are mad at your mother for being mentally unstable! You're the one who is mentally unstable!" Maggie shouted as she laced her fingers around the leg of the bed. She could see Robert's feet. When he knelt, her heart jumped into her throat.

Like a wild animal, he grabbed at her ankles. Maggie kicked and kicked while holding on tight.

"Maggie! Tell me where the records are!"

"I don't know! Even if I did, I wouldn't tell you! You don't deserve to hold office!" Maggie shouted as she kicked with all her strength.

Just then, she heard a loud slam from downstairs.

"Yo, Robert! Where are you?" It was Rich Murphy.

Robert stopped trying to grab Maggie and jumped to his feet.

"No! Rich! Don't come up here!" Maggie screamed. "He'll kill you too!"

"What?" Rich called as he crossed the foyer.

"Get out of here, Rich! Run!" Maggie shouted, only to have Robert's loud stomps across the wooden floor drown her out. Panting, she watched as Robert darted out the door.

Without wasting any time, Maggie pulled her sweaty hands from the rope and flung it aside as if it was a snake that had been coiled around her wrists, ready to strike. She began to scoot out from under the bed only to feel something sharp cut across her belly as she slid along the floor—an old metal latch. Maggie swallowed even though her mouth had gone dry.

Maggie heard Rich talking downstairs. He was going on about something she couldn't make out when suddenly, he shouted. "Hey, man! What do you think you're doing? Get away from me, man! Hey, I did what you asked! You don't need to…"

There was a grunt. A thud. Silence. Then footsteps that Maggie recognized. She scrambled out from under the bed and lunged at the door, slamming it shut and snapping the lock into place just in time.

There was a princess phone on the nightstand. Maggie's heart leapt, but when she lifted the receiver, she wanted to spit; she heard no dial tone.

Robert started pounding on the door. He was

yelling something about how they could have a lovely life together. How he knew that once she showed him where his family's records of mental health problems were located, they could live happily ever after. It would all be their secret. The psychotic episodes, the voices in his head, and the tragedies of Mom, Shelly, and Brian could all be forgotten.

"It'll be like they never happened, Maggie. You must trust me! I won't hurt you! I promise!" With each sentence, Robert banged against the door.

Maggie looked around the room and saw the closet, an elaborate wooden wardrobe, and the windows. There was no place she could hide. No place at all.

You don't need to hide. You need to escape, her mind ordered.

Maggie tore apart the curtains and pushed up the window. When she stuck her head out, she saw she was facing the street, and there was no trellis. No ivy to cling to. But there was a part of the roof, slick with moisture from the earlier rain and slowly turning to ice as the temperature started to drop.

I can't. I'll break my neck for sure. No one will ever know what happened to me. They'll think I was chasing after a cat or maybe had nothing more to say than "Goodbye, cruel world."

But the pounding on the door behind her sounded the alarm that she had to do something. With each thrust, Robert was getting closer and closer to busting the door open. The doorknob lock wasn't like a dead bolt or padlock. It was flimsy in comparison, and the sound of the wood around the doorframe cracking was proof. Maggie had no choice.

As she swung one leg over the sill and planted her foot on the slick shingles, she was sure she could hear voices. Part of her wanted to start screaming. Another part of her wanted to shrink away into nothingness out of sheer humiliation. But the dry fracture of the door frame prodded her into action. Robert had bust through the door. Just as she pulled her other leg out the window, he launched himself, flailing his arms in a mad attempt to get hold of her.

"Get back here, Maggie! You'll kill yourself!"

"You were going to kill me! Don't you see the irony in that statement?" she shouted as she dropped to her knees and crawled slowly in the direction of the porch. If she could manage to get to it, she might be able to shimmy down the porch posts. However, it wouldn't take Robert but a few seconds to run through the house and out the front door to get her. Still, she was safer here than she was in the house. At least, she thought she was.

Everything looked the same in the dark. One section of roof looked identical to another. But as Maggie placed her hand on a patch of shingles, she could feel them give slightly beneath her. The sound of soft wood grinding against itself as it bent downward made Maggie's stomach flip. The roof was old and rotten underneath. Any sudden move might send her plummeting through the framework only to thud against the hardwood or shag carpeting in the room below. She didn't know what was down there, but Maggie was keenly aware she'd break every bone in her body if the roof gave way.

"Maggie!" Robert began to climb out the window.

"No! Don't! Robert! The roof can't hold us both! Stop!" Maggie shouted as she slowly and carefully inched toward the flatter part of the porch roof. By now, she was sure she could hear voices. So she kept shouting "no" and "don't." But Robert didn't listen.

Her knees felt as if she'd been crawling across rows of pencils. Grit and grime coated her hands.

She thought of the pretty outfit she'd put on, never dreaming that it would be ruined like this.

"Maggie! Get over here!" Robert growled.

Her breath was coming in short bursts. If she didn't make a move now, Robert would overcome her. All he'd have to do is give her a shove off the roof and claim she had done it to herself. He'd tried to stop her but…

After a gulp of air, a few blinks of her eyes to focus, and a quick prayer, Maggie pushed herself up and teetered like a child learning to walk to the flatter part of the roof. However, setting foot on it, she realized it was even softer that the roof of the main house. Without thinking, she pushed herself up on her tiptoes. It wasn't logical, but for some reason, it made her feel like she might be relieving some of the strain on the shingles. Like a tightrope walker, her arms stretched out, her eyes glued to the space in front of her, she hurried to the edge of the porch and peered over.

You climbed down the side of a building once today. You can do it again, her little voice encouraged.

Maggie was glad she couldn't see the contents of the gutter as she took hold of it. It was full of freezing mush, but it gave her something to hold on to as she swung one leg over.

Of course, she was too short to reach the porch banister. Her arms were not strong enough for her to dangle over the edge for long. But when she looked up, she saw Robert getting closer. Would he step on her fingers? Would he kick her off the roof? She swung her other leg over. Her weight began to put a strain on the gutter, and it began to pull away from the siding.

This is it. I'm going to fall and break my neck. And if I somehow manage to live, Robert is going to come to the hospital and smother me with a pillow. Either way, it's the end, Maggie thought as the sound of metal and nails scraping together echoed across the driveway.

Suddenly, Maggie felt a pair of strong arms around her waist. She was yanked onto the porch. She tumbled backward and landed squarely on top of a man who grunted as all the wind was knocked out of him.

"Oh my gosh." Maggie squinted. "Rich? Are you okay?"

"You're heavier than you look," Rich Murphy muttered, blinking as blood trickled from his nose.

Chapter 21

"**C**ome on. You've got to get up," Maggie urged, clumsily getting to her feet and taking Rich by the hand. "He's crazy. Robert has gone totally nuts."

"He's always been this way," Rich said. "It's about time it all stopped."

"What?" Maggie stared.

In the faint light, Maggie saw Rich looking past her. She whirled around to see two legs dangling over the side of the porch roof. Her heart stopped. She died for a second. She was sure of it. Everything froze, and she suddenly realized how much of her life she'd wasted. What was she waiting for? The world was a big place, and she could see any of it she wanted. There was more to life than books and coffee. Why hadn't she dated Joshua Whitfield by now? What was she waiting for? But now it seemed like it was too late.

Robert dropped down with a thud.

When nothing more than a squeak escaped her lips, Maggie felt those strong arms again push her aside. Rich stepped between her and Robert.

"It's over, man." Rich's head bobbed up and down. "I can't live with myself. You are on your own, Bob. But you aren't going to do anything to Maggie. She doesn't know anything."

"She does so. Shelly had her name and specifically made reference to speaking with her during this reunion. She does know and…"

"It's your paranoia, Bob. Shelly wanted to apologize to Maggie for the way she treated her in high school. It's step number nine, dude. It had been eating away at her for some time. She wanted to make things right. Maggie doesn't know where anything is in your mother's house. Neither do I. I should never have gone along with you. I should never have had that first drink," Rich said. His shoulders slumped a little.

Robert shook with anger and cold. Behind him, the faint glow of red and blue lights grew until two squad cars pulled into the driveway. Maggie thought the sound of Gary's voice yelling for everyone to get their hands up sounded like that of an angel. She was sure that Robert was going to make one last stand and maybe grab her or Rich as some kind of hostage or getaway ticket.

But he didn't. Instead, he walked over to a corner of the porch, pressed his back against the siding, and slid to the floor. He stayed there while Maggie and Rich walked to the police cars.

"Mags? I should have known," Gary said, pulling her away from Rich and quickly grabbing a blanket from his trunk to wrap her in.

"He's crazy, Gary. How did you know to come?" Maggie asked as she pulled the blanket tight around her shoulders.

"The neighbors called and said there were some kids vandalizing the house," Gary replied. "What happened?"

"I thought he wanted to take me out for Valentine's Day," Maggie said.

She wasn't sure if the tears that surfaced in her eyes were from relief now that she was safe or sadness that she wasn't really anyone's Valentine. With a deep breath, she choked back her emotions and told Gary all the strange things Robert had said.

By this time, the other officer had collected Robert from the porch. He didn't put up any fuss as they escorted him to the car and placed him in the back seat.

"What was he talking about?" Gary asked.

That was when Maggie remembered the scrape on her stomach when she was under the bed. She led Gary up the stairs to Robert's mother's room. They pushed the bed aside, and sure enough, there was a small trapdoor beneath it. Maggie flipped the latch and pulled it open.

"Robert said his mother had these cubbies all over the house," Maggie said. She pulled out a folder that was wrapped in a dried rubber band that crumbled as soon as she touched it. When she opened the folder, the first words she read were *Snowfall Valley Psychiatric Hospital*. Beneath it were the name Josephine Hallas and the word *admittance*.

As Maggie flipped through the documents, they became older and older, with different first names, yet all with the last name Hallas and a long list of mental facilities they'd each spent time in.

"There was a history of mental illness in the family," Maggie said. "That's why he went to live with his father after their divorce. And Robert wanted to hide the mental illness so he could run for office."

"Right. Name a family that doesn't have some kind of mental illness in it. I had an uncle who thought he was Saint Gerome. Didn't stop him from going to work every day."

Maggie took a deep breath. "Rich said Shelly was going to apologize to me for how she acted in school. Part of her twelve-step program." Maggie stood and handed the Hallas family records to Gary. "But Robert killed her because she wouldn't or couldn't give these to him. He did his mother in too. He said so. Gary, is Robert insane, or is he just... selfish?"

"I don't know, Maggie. That will be for the professionals to decide."

"Shelly had said she wanted to talk to me at the reunion. I wonder if we could have been friends. I wonder if she could have gotten better and started her life over. My gosh, we have dozens of self-help books at the bookstore. Why didn't she say some-thing sooner? Maybe this could have been avoided."

"Maggie, you can't go thinking any of this was your fault. It happened, and now we have to let the law even things out. Okay?" Gary put his hand on

Maggie's shoulder. "Everyone knew how jealous Shelly was of you. She could do a million steps and read a million books, and she'd never come close to being the kind of lady you are."

"I wish people would stop saying that. It doesn't make any sense," Maggie said, wrinkling her nose and pulling her blanket more tightly over her shoulders.

"Someday, maybe you'll see what the rest of us see, Mags," Gary replied. "Come on. I'll drive you home."

"I'd like nothing better, but I'm still at Mrs. Burnside's B&B."

"No. I ran into Mrs. Peacock. She said your place is clean. No bedbugs," Gary whispered.

"Really? Oh, thank goodness." Again, Maggie felt like crying. What a relief it would be to rest in her own bed with her own teacups and her own books with her own radio to play some quiet music, safe and sound in her tiny cottage.

As they walked outside, Maggie asked Gary what was going to happen to Rich Murphy.

"I'm not sure. We'll have to get his statement. See how much he was involved. Brian O'Keefe is going to recover, so we'll have more questions for him and his involvement. But from what I can gather, those two were nothing but useful idiots," Gary said.

"That sounds about right. But Rich did help me. If it weren't for him, I don't know what would have happened," Maggie said as they drove to her house.

She had a key under her mat and wasn't going to worry about picking up her things at the B&B until the next day.

As she reached the front door, Mrs. Peacock called out. Maggie turned around. Her feet were freezing and her knees ached terribly, but she was happy to see Mrs. Peacock nonetheless.

"Oh, I'm glad you got word, dear. Yes, the houses are both devoid of bedbugs. You have no idea what a weight this is off my shoulders. The hotel was costing me a fortune, and when you are on a fixed budget, every penny counts," Mrs. Peacock said without a "Hello" or "How are you?"

"Yes, I'm sure," Maggie replied. "Mrs. Peacock, I wanted to thank you for the clothes you bought for me. Everything was so beautiful and fit just perfectly. I know you didn't want me to say anything, but I just had to say thanks."

Maggie stood there for a moment, waiting for Mrs. Peacock to wave her leather-gloved hand or roll her heavily made-up eyes. Instead, she looked at Maggie as if she had a bedbug on the tip of her nose.

"Dear, what are you talking about?"

"The clothes you bought me. Because I couldn't retrieve anything from the cottage because of the exterminators. This blouse." Maggie pulled back her jacket. "The shoes. The outfit I wore for the reunion. You bought them for me. Didn't you?"

"Margaret, I'm on a fixed budget. I can barely afford clothes for myself. I didn't buy you anything," Mrs. Peacock replied.

"Oh." Maggie bit her lip and furrowed her brow. Mrs. Peacock prattled on about a few more things and then waved goodbye as she headed back up to the main house.

Maggie went inside, shut the door behind her, and snapped the dead bolt into place. She flipped on the light and saw everything just as she'd left it. It was good to be home.

But as comfortable as she was in her own bed, after a hot cup of tea and with the radio playing some soft classical music, Maggie couldn't sleep. It was as if she was just counting down the minutes until she could unlock the front door at the Bookish Café.

When she finally did, wearing one of her favorite outfits she'd bought herself, a purple blazer with a white blouse and wide-legged pants, she waited for Joshua to arrive.

"Morning, Mags," he said. He was wearing one of his many flannel shirts and blue jeans, with a tool belt hanging on his hips.

"Morning, Joshua."

"You look nice this morning," he said as he stood in front of the thermostat, tinkering with the dial.

The memory of the previous evening, crawling across a cold, wet roof with a maniac behind her and unstable shingles beneath her, made Maggie do something she would have never done in a million years before last night. But so much about life was unpredictable. So she walked around the counter and up to Joshua and wrapped her arms around his neck. She wanted to give him a kiss. She wanted nothing more than to feel his soft lips against hers. But at the last second, she nestled her head in his neck and, instead, opted for a big, tight hug.

"Thank you," she replied.

To her surprise, Joshua hugged her back just as tightly. "You're welcome," he whispered in her ear. They pulled apart.

Maggie quickly looked down at her feet then slipped behind the counter again and began organizing her money in the cash drawer. "Yeah, fix that thermostat. It's chilly in here all the time," she said.

"It's the same temperature as the café. It's not chilly," Joshua replied, turning his back to her to face the thermostat again.

As Maggie watched him, she could see the smile on his face even if he wasn't looking at her. She smiled, too, but wasn't ready to let him see it either.

About the Author

Harper Lin is a *USA TODAY* bestselling cozy mystery author. When she's not reading or writing mysteries, she loves going to yoga classes, hiking, and hanging out with her family and friends.

For a complete list of her books by series, visit her website. Follow Harper on social media using the icons below for the latest insider news.

www.HarperLin.com

www.ingramcontent.com/pod-product-compliance
Lightning Source LLC
Chambersburg PA
CBHW052043240626
47153CB00006B/2196